DOCTAROO
AND THE GUY WITH THE
GOLDEN GNU

Based on the PWC spoof television serial

PAUL MACEOGHAIN

I0684756

A DARTBOARD BOOK

Published by

the Paperback Division of

LITTLEFILMS Ltd.

Copyright: Paul MacEoghain 2020

ISBN 978-0-244-27557-0

Chapter One

A Tuesday morning in Hyde Park is much like every other morning in Hyde Park. Pigeons, Gulls and Starlings vie for attention from the tourists and joggers, each expecting seed, corn or the odd sandwich corner thrown to them by sightseers. However, this particular Tuesday was slightly different. The gulls had flown off to Margate, the pigeons had decided just to hang around Trafalgar Square and the starlings had discovered a garden in Beckenham where a little old lady had put out some fat balls and one of those suet-filled half coconut shells. The reason for this was that someone had parked an old, red Telephone Box on the grass near Prince's Gate. The door was open and an odd mixture of people came out.

There were four of them. Their leader was a woman who, to all intents and purposes, appeared to be in her late thirties with short blonde hair and horn-rimmed glasses perched precariously on a squat, slightly bulbous nose. She wore a pale blue T-Shirt with the logo of the children's television programme "Rainbow" on the chest, denim Capri pants and a pink woolen cardigan draped across her shoulders. This was the thirteenth Doctaroo, who this time resembled a certain north east of England comedian. She turned to the first of her companions who was a man in late middle age with short grey slightly receding hair; a lined but nonetheless kind face and wearing comfortable brown corduroy slacks and cozy Fair Isle sweater.

"Howay Mr. Walsh, pet. We're back in your old stomping grounds."

Mr. Walsh turned up his nose and sniffed the air.

"Ah, yes. There's nothing like the smell of diesel and doner kebab meat to bring back the memories."

Doctaroo sniffed too.

"Doner kebab? Yeah, well, if it's been eaten by a Rottweiler first and then pooped out..."

"It's an acquired taste," muttered Mr. Walsh and he stomped off in a huff.

"Big baby," came a shrill voice, like fingernails down a blackboard, except with a thick Liverpudlian accent.

"You'd think he owned the place the way he goes on about it."

The person who owned the voice was a petite red head with huge false eyelashes Like two upside down spiders has decided to have a rest on top of her eyes and who wore a short monochrome mini skirt. This was Beryl, a chirpy, perky scouser. You know, one of the annoying ones who say they won't do anything because, "oh no, I'd feel ashamed..." but who then do it anyway because it was their idea in the first place. The sort you really,

really wanted to hit with a dishcloth. Wrapped around a breezeblock.

"Leave him alone," came a gentle voice from behind. Brian brought up the rear of the group. He was six feet two of pure, rippling, unadulterated flab. We are talking zero muscle mass and 100% ragu sauce.

He was an art student from Bethnal Green who dressed like David Baddiel used to in the 90s. The only problem was that he was from 2018.

"You're only defending him 'cos you're in love with him," shot back Beryl.

"I'm not in love with him," complained Brian, pulling a Twinkie he'd found from his coat pocket.

"I just think he's an interesting and sensitive man," he said picking bits of pocket fluff off the sponge cake before stuffing it into his mouth.

Beryl gave him a disgusted look. "You've just shoved a whole Twinkie in yer gob in one go. You big fat cu..."

"That's enough," interrupted Doctaroo. This is a PG rated book. We don't want an R rating.

"I'm hungry," complained Brian. "Is there a Greggs nearby?"

"Here you go, pet," said Doctaroo passing Brian a squished-up Mars bar she'd rooted from her cardigan pocket. "It's a bit manky, mind. I'm not sure how long it's been there."

Brian snatched the proffered confectionery and greedily stuffed it into his mouth.

"Actually," Doctaroo said sheepishly, "I think it's been in there since I got my cardi."

"Ewww," squeezed Beryl. "Didn't you buy it from a charity shop?"

"Oh, no pet," Doctaroo corrected her. "I got it from a jumble sale in 1977. I remember it 'cos it was the Queen's Silver Jubilee and there was a street party afterwards."

"Ugh, Brian! You've just scoffed a chocolate bar from 1977!" Beryl laughed at him. "You're dead gross."

"Don't care," said Brian between bouts of furious chewing. 'Tastes goooood."

"Do you mind?" Said Mr Walsh, impatiently, "Some of us are in a hurry."

"Liar," scoffed Beryl. "You're the only one in a hurry. *We've* gorrall the time in the world."

"Look young lady," said Mr Walsh striding up to her.

"I had to put up with your little jaunt to Jupiter to watch the moonsrise last week. *And* I had to sit through that Alanis Morrissette concert you and Brian wanted to see. Even though you spent the entire gig throwing Tori Amos CDs at the stage and shouting, '…hey Alanis, that's ironic!' at her. Now it's *my* turn."

"Alright granddad, keep yer wig on!" Beryl retorted "No need to go off the deep end."
Mr Walsh glared at her, then walked away.

"Howay, you two. We've got company."

Doctaroo had stopped walking and was staring at a group of about half a dozen police officers that had arranged themselves in a semi-circle in front of them. Six more were approaching them from the left and a further six from the right. Brian and Beryl turned back the way they had come only to find that another group of six was approaching from the rear.

All were armed with Glock 17s and were pointing them in Doctaroo's general direction.

"Oooh," said Doctaroo appreciatively. "I love a man in uniform."

Mr. Walsh raised his hands above his head and the others followed suit. Doctaroo had trotted over to the nearest officer and was happily taking selfies with the embarrassed copper. She was trying to clamber up into his arms when a tall, thin, officious looking bloke in a light grey, tailored suit pushed his way to the front of the group of police officers.

"Are you Doctaroo?" He asked Mr. Walsh.
Mr. Walsh pointed at the apparently sex-mad woman who was attempting to stick her tongue down the throat of the mortified, yet obviously slightly aroused young bobby. The suit hurried over to the officer's aid.

"Madam, please! I insist you desist!" He pulled her off the constable with considerable difficulty and ordered him to rejoin his colleagues. Doctaroo wasn't impressed.

"Here, pet. You forgot to give me your number," she called after him. The constable all but ran back to the relative safety of his fellow officers.

"Don't worry, hinny," she trilled, "you can give it to me later. And I'll get your number at the same time."

"Doctaroo, I really must insist!" yelled the suit. Doctaroo looked him up and down and snorted.

"You can insist all you like love, there's no way I'd want *your* number!"

"Doctaroo, please..." began the suit, but Doctaroo interrupted him.

"There's no point in begging either. I just don't go for weirdos in suits. Well, not after that incident with that footballer and the Rigellian Ambassador, anyway. Took me *ages* to get the stains out."

"Look, Doctaroo. My name is Nigel Maule-Ffinch; I work for the Home Office. I've been asked to escort you to Scotland Yard."

"Whaddya wannus to go to Scottie Yard for, Nigel?" spoke up Beryl.

"I beg your pardon?"

"She means," replied Mr. Walsh, "why do you want us at Scotland Yard, Mr. Maule-Ffinch?"

"Alright, granddad," said Beryl indignantly. "I can fight me own battles you know."

"You'd have to," muttered Mr. Walsh.

"Because they wouldn't understand a bloody word you're saying otherwise."

He ducked as a stiletto-heeled shoe flew over his head. There was a muffled "Ow!" As it collided with the luckless police officer that Doctaroo had earlier set her sights on.

"Sorry..." Beryl called out. "Can I have me shoe back please?" The young copper walked cautiously over, shoe in hand. Beryl took it and slipped it back onto her foot.

Maule-Ffinch cleared his throat.

"Right, well. If you would all like to come with me please. We have arranged special transport to take you to Scotland Yard."

"Well, it had better be something special," said Doctaroo as she followed him to the exit, slipping her hand through the young police officer's arm in the process. "I'm a girl with expensive tastes..." she lowered her voice to a seductive whisper. "...if you know what I mean, pet."

The officer's face went the same colour as the London Transport bus that awaited them on the road outside the park gates. Maule-Ffinch opened the door and gestured them inside.

"What?" said Brian. "Is this what you call 'special'? A double-decker bus?"

"It's inconspicuous," said Maule-Ffinch. "There are certain parties from whom we don't want to draw attention."

Doctaroo happily hopped on board the bus and dragging the police officer along with her, made her way to the back and plonked herself down on the vinyl seat. Mr. Walsh came next, followed by Beryl and finally Brian, who reluctantly sat down on the disabled seat at the front.

Beryl poked him in the back. "Hey, you. You can't sit there."

Brian frowned at her. "Why not?"

"Cos it's for the cripples, that's why!" Beryl said indignantly.

"Okay," sighed Brian. "For one thing, we don't call them cripples 'cos it's offensive, inaccurate and wrong, and for another, *we're the only ones on board the bus!*" Brian rolled his eyes and stretched out on the seat.

Maule-Finch sat down in front of Doctaroo. He turned and gave a gentle cough to attract her attention from her in-depth, oral re-examination of the constable's tonsils.

"Excuse me, Doctaroo?"

Doctaroo grunted, not wanting to turn away from the task-in-hand. Maule-Ffinch went on.

"If you could stop doing that for a moment, please?"

Doctaroo made it clear that stopping wasn't something she intended to do any time soon. Maule-Ffinch, although taken aback by the gesture Doctaroo had made in his direction, carried on regardless.

"Doctaroo, I really must insist on you releasing Constable Perkins."

Doctaroo stopped kissing him and glanced sideways at Maule-Ffinch.

"Why?"

"Because," stammered Maule-Ffinch. "He's our driver."

"Oh," said Doctaroo. "Oh well in that case..." She relaxed her grip on the constable and he hurriedly stood up, smoothing down his uniform. He gave Maule-Ffinch a grateful smile and quickly made his way to the driver's cab.

"Don't forget, you owe me dinner later," Doctaroo shouted after him. "And I want to go somewhere posh," she called, "like Weatherspoon's."

Chapter Two.

Perkins settled himself in the driver's seat and started the engine. It roared into life with a sound not usually heard outside of a track day at Brands Hatch. Clearly, the bus had been considerably upgraded and Perkins smiled at the vibrations coming from the steering wheel. A fan of muscle cars from a young age, Perkins was certain that, from the steady throb-throb he felt, the bus now hid nothing less than a turbocharged V16 engine under its bonnet. Probably. He looked around him and noticed that in addition to about half a dozen cup holders, there was also a brand new Blaupunkt fitted snugly into the dashboard. There was a CD on top of the dash and he popped it into the player. He put the gear stick into 'Drive' and flicking on the indicators, pulled out onto the bus lane. Grinning happily, Perkins applied a little more pressure onto the accelerator pedal and the bus went from zero to forty in less time than it takes a fat bloke to find the buffet at a christening.

At the back, Maule-Ffinch was trying vainly to explain to Doctaroo, Beryl, Brian and a worried Mr. Walsh, why they were being summoned to Scotland Yard. Beryl was clearly bored, Brian was stuffing his face with a half-eaten slice of pepperoni pizza he'd found wedges down the back of his seat and Doctaroo was too busy trying to attract Perkins' attention in his rear-view mirror to listen to what Maule-Ffinch had to say. Only Mr. Walsh was paying him any heed.

"...so, you see," Maule-Ffinch was saying, "in a nutshell, that's why we need your help. Of course, the Chief Inspector will brief you properly;

I'm just here to give you the 'heads up', so to speak."

It was obvious that Maule-Ffinch had derived a great deal of pleasure from using the term, as the joy in which he said the words 'heads up' was written large on his face and he beamed happily at Doctaroo.

"Hmm? What's that, hinnie?" She said absently, gazing up the bus at Perkins' reflection. Maule-Ffinch's face fell.

"I, I, I," stammered Maule-Ffinch. "I was just telling you why the Home Office sent me..."

"Oh right." Smiled Doctaroo, diverting her attention back to the flustered civil servant. "And why's that then?"

Maule-Ffinch stared at her, mouth agape. "Didn't you listen to anything I said?" he said quietly.

"Oh, aye," she said, "I heard the bit about us going to Scotland Yard, but after that I sorta drifted off. It's not your fault pet. You shouldn't blame yourself."

"Some people are good at tellin' stories and some aren't. Isn't that right Doctaroo?" said Beryl weighing in with her two-pennorth. "I don't think you're cut out to be a storyteller, Nige."

Maule-Ffinch opened his mouth to reply, thought better of it and closed it, then reconsidered and opened it again.

Beryl was looking out the window at the city, its people rushing here and there and generally doing what people usually do first thing in the morning in London. She shook her head in wonder. Doctaroo smiled at her.

"Something wrong, pet?" she asked gently. Beryl shook her head.

"No, it's just that..."

"Just that what, petal?" Doctaroo enquired.

"I came to London once. Back in '59 I think it was," Beryl said. "With me Aunty Val and our Elaine. We stayed at a swanky hotel and went to the theatre to see a play."

"Ooh, sounds lovely. What play did you see?"

Beryl turned to look at Doctaroo. "It was a dead serious one with that Alan Bates bloke in it. Me Aunty Val fancied him like mad. *Look Back in Anger* I think it was called."

"Wasn't that a song by Oasis?" asked Brian.

"No," said Doctaroo. "You're thinking of Wonderwall."

"Prefer Wham myself," piped up Mr. Walsh.

"Ooh, yes!" said Doctaroo enthusiastically. "I love a bit o' Wham!"

"Wake me up before you go-go," said Mr. Walsh.

"Aww, are you getting your head down for a bit? That's nice."

There was a sudden flash of flame from the driver's cab followed by a loud bang and a billow of smoke from the dashboard. The bus suddenly accelerated and swerved out of the bus lane and into traffic, causing whatever Maule-Ffinch was about to say next to immediately vanish from his mind, replaced by blind panic and a primal whimper he

19

later couldn't even remember making. In an instant Brian was on his feet, but realising that this caused a sudden rush of blood to nip down to his legs, making him feel giddy and light-headed. He sat down again.

The bus swerved alarmingly across the road into oncoming traffic. Mr. Walsh dived forward and hoisting the unfortunate Constable Perkins from the driver's seat, he quickly took his place and tried to wrestle the bus back into the bus lane. He pumped the brake pedal with his foot, but to no avail.

"We've got no brakes!" he yelled to no one in particular. "How do you stop a double decker bus with no brakes?"

"Oh, I know this one," Doctaroo called out. "I'm sure it was a question on Who Wants to be a Millionaire last week..."

"Well?" Mr. Walsh called back. "What was the answer?"

"I dunno," Doctaroo shrugged. "The adverts came on and I went to make a cuppa. Shall I phone a friend?"

"Can they fix a bus?"

20

"No. But they fixed a puncture on my bike once."

"Oh good," said Mr. Walsh sarcastically. "I'll know who to call if the tyres blow then, won't I?"

There was a bang from the front left corner of the bus and it swerved suddenly into the kerb. Mr. Walsh struggled with the steering wheel.

"What was your friend's number?" he shouted over his shoulder.

Maule-Ffinch shook his head and recovered his composure. Grabbing onto the handrail, he staggered up the bus to the cab.

"Try the handbrake."

"I have," said Mr. Walsh. "It's not working either."

"How about turning off the engine?" Maule-Ffinch suggested. Mr. Walsh nodded and reached out to grab the key. As he touched it, there was a spark of electricity and he snatched back his hand and sucked his fingers.

"I'm not doing that again, mate," he said in alarm.

Maule-Ffinch scanned the road ahead. Approximately five hundred or so yards in front of them, the road was coned off and the traffic was down to a single lane.

"It looks like there's roadworks up ahead," he said. "You're going to have to crash the bus."

"What?" shouted Mr. Walsh. "Are you crazy?"

"Possibly. My therapist says I have narcissistic personality disorder. I think he's just saying that because I'm so much better at everything than he is. Anyway, look ahead to where they're digging up the road, do you see those barrels?"

Mr. Walsh nodded. "Yeah, I see them."

"Good," said Maule-Ffinch. "They're filled with water. I want you to drive into them, they should cushion the impact."

Mr. Walsh stared at him as though he'd just asked him to paint his bum green and hide in a supermarket's fruit and veg aisle and pretend to be a watermelon.

"Are you on tablets for your condition?" he asked through gritted teeth.

22

"Well, yes actually, I am," replied Maule-Ffinch.

"Good," said Mr. Walsh steering the bus towards the barrels of water. "Get them to increase your dose!"

Aleksey Błażejewski had only been working for Westminster Council for a fortnight and he was enjoying his job immensely.

His current task was to oversee the repairs to a stretch of the road near Hyde Park Corner and he was proud of the work he and his team were doing. They had recently dug up part of the road to allow a cable television company access to the fibre optic cables that ran around six feet underground.

What he expected was a slight disruption to the local traffic.

What he expected was the job to go without a hitch.

What he expected was to be finished well within the estimated time of completion.

What he didn't expect was a big, red, double-decker bus to come careering along the bus lane and smash through the barrels, finishing up front first in the hole they had recently dug. The last thing Aleksey Błażejewski saw before the nearside wing mirror clipped him and sent him flying backwards and crashing into a pile of recently unearthed rubble, was the terrified face of a retired librarian from Penge.

It was, thought Aleksey Błażejewski as his eyes closed for what would be the last time in his relatively short life, completely unexpected.

Brian slowly opened his eyes and cautiously took in his surroundings. Doctaroo was tentatively getting to her feet; simultaneously checking for any injuries and helping Beryl pick herself up from where she had fallen. Mr. Walsh was extricating himself from the driver's cab and, stepping over the late constable Perkins' body, hurried over to where Maule-Ffinch lay in the doorwell. Brian clambered over to them.

"Are you okay, Mr. Walsh?" he asked in concern. Mr. Walsh nodded.

"Yeah, I'm fine. Pity I can't say the same for poor old Perkins over there though." He gestured backwards with his thumb.

Brian moved over to the body, wincing as he saw the CD embedded in his forehead. "Blimey, that stereo packed a wallop, eh?"

"Oh, my poor Perkins." Cried Doctaroo, clambering over the seats to where the late constable lay. "Oh, pet, no."

"Killed by compact disc," said Mr. Walsh sadly.

"Aww, that's so sad," Beryl cried. "What CD was it?"

Brian bent over Perkins' body and read the disc's title. "Er, Phil Collins' Greatest Hits."

"Oh, no. That's terrible." Cried Doctaroo.

"You're telling *me*!" said a shocked Brian.

"Aye," said Doctaroo. "You'd have thought it'd be something decent like Steps or Jive Bunny."

Chapter Three.

"Not far now," said Maule-Ffinch. At thirty-four, he felt that he had his life on track. He had a steady job, prospects, and a beautiful boyfriend. Maule-Ffinch considered himself extremely lucky. He reckoned that he was okay looking, albeit in a slightly crooked Jimmy Carr sort of way. He had all his own teeth and hair, both of which were immaculate and looked after.

He had inherited a minor title and a nine-figure fortune from his father and his job had taken him around the world many times. He had dined in some of the world's finest restaurants, stayed in the best hotels and counted numerous celebrities and heads-of-state as close friends.

Yes, life was good. Except for one thing: This sodding assignment.

He had read the Home Office's file on Doctaroo, of course. Taken in every detail. His/her quirks, his/her eccentricities. However, nothing had prepared him for his/her latest persona. This latest persona was strolling along by his side and talking incessantly about subjects of which he had zero knowledge or interest. Nevertheless, he nodded, smiled and laughed politely at the points where he believed she expected him to.

"...so, there we were," she was saying, "trapped on a spaceship with an alien that fed on nostalgia. Poor Mr. Walsh was nearly completely drained. If it hadn't for Brian's quick thinking and searching for '80s telly on YouTube, he might not have survived."

"Really? How interesting..." he began. Doctaroo cut him off.

"And then, another time, I'd landed on a planet populated by a race of people who worshipped Simon Cowell! Can you imagine?" she broke off into a fit of giggles. "They all had spray tans too!"

"Gosh, is that so? How…"

"Then there was the time I visited a planet inhabited by a race of invisible meerkats." She held up a hand to prevent him from speaking.

"Go on," she said with an impish smile. "Ask me how I knew they were meerkats if they were invisible?"

Maule-Ffinch looked blankly at her for a moment then opened his mouth to speak. "Ah, um, erm… How do you know…?"

Before he could finish his sentence, she jumped in and gave him a sly grin before laughing loudly. "It's SIMPLES!!!" He winced as she nudged him sharply in the ribs. "Get it? Simples! They're meerkats!" she sighed. "Oh, that's funny."

"Yes," stammered Maul-Finch.

New Scotland Yard, the headquarters of London's Metropolitan Police Force, is situated in the former Curtis Green Building, the third of three buildings that comprised its first home on the Victoria Embankment and the Met had moved into the newly constructed building in 1890 after relocating there from the old Great Scotland Yard building at 4 Whitehall Place. A second building was added in 1906 and the third in 1940. The force moved again in 1967 to Victoria Broadway, before finally returning to its original home in 2016.

Nigel Maule-Ffinch led his tired and bedraggled companions up the steps and through the doors of the main entrance and up to the main reception desk. The officer on duty looked him up and down.

"Afternoon, Mr Finch. We were expecting you this morning," he said wryly.

Maule-Ffinch winced inwardly at the officer's mispronunciation of his name

"We were delayed somewhat," he said in the most officious way he could muster. "Please inform Chief Inspector Carstairs of our arrival."

The desk sergeant leaned forward slightly and gave him an evil-looking smile, all crooked teeth and nicotine-stained lips.

"He's been waiting for you since ten this morning. Which is when you should have got here. He's not best pleased with *you*."

"Just tell me where he is please, *Sergeant*!" Maule-Ffinch said, emphasising the word sergeant in an 'I can soon arrange for you to be pounding the beat again *constable*' kind of way.

The sergeant stopped smiling and gave Maule-Ffinch a look of pure hatred.

"Fifth floor briefing room. First left out the lift, second door along."

"Thank you," Nigel said and bustled Doctaroo and her friends towards one of the glass lifts. Suddenly, he stopped and turned around. He marched back to the reception and banged his fist on the desk in front of the sergeant.

"And it's *Maule-Ffinch*! So, don't you bloody well forget it!" he shouted. "It's bloody Maule-*Ffinch*! Two. Bloody. Fs! *F-Finch*!" His voice broke as he screamed out the last word and it came out like a squeaky falsetto. He banged unconvincingly on the desk with his fist again, turned quickly on his heel and strode unconfidently back to where Brian was holding open the lift door for him.

As he entered, Doctaroo gave him a reassuring smile. "Well done, pet. That told him."

They rode up through the building in relative silence, apart from the occasional sniff and a stifled giggle from Beryl at one point, when all the junk food Brian had been stuffing his face with resulted in an unfortunate build up and subsequent release of flatulence from his nether regions.

Doctaroo wrinkled up her nose at the noxious odour emanating from her companion. "Howay, pet," she said, covering her nose with her hand. "Something's crawled up your arse and died!"

"Sorry," mumbled an embarrassed Brian, letting out another odious guff. "Must have been those sprouts I ate at lunch time."

"Aye," said Doctaroo, wafting the smell towards Mr Walsh who pinched his nose and breathed through his mouth before realising he could actually *taste* it.

"And the rest," she continued. "You haven't stopped since yesterday."

"Jeez, Brian. Can't you just stick a cork up yer bum?" muttered Beryl. "It's bad enough you waited 'till   we were in the soddin' lift before you farted."

"Eee," giggled Doctaroo. "This reminds me of the time I was stuck in a lift with that American singer bloke. Ooh, what was his name again? He's married to one of those lovely Kardashian girls..."

"Kanye West?" replied Brian.

"Dunno," said Doctaroo with a grin, "I've never wested before."

"No," said an exasperated Brian. The rapper."

"Ohhh!" exclaimed Doctaroo. "I see what you mean now!" She winked at Maule-Ffinch. "No, pet, I always take the wrapper off first."

She burst into fits of laughter, nudging first Beryl, who joined in with a cackle and then Mr Walsh, who didn't. The lift stopped and disgorged its contents onto the fifth floor where they were met by a tanned, handsome man in his late fifties.

He was wearing a stylish, Italian cut Armani suit in a tasteful bluish-grey, over a crisp pale grey Hugo Boss shirt and finished by a shiny pair of black Gucci lace-up brogues. His greying hair was Brylcreemed and swept back from the temples and gathered in a ridiculous little pony tail at the back of his head.

Detective Chief Inspector Cedric Carstairs was a fourth-generation copper who had joined the force straight from Oxford where he'd earned a double first in Criminology and Criminal Justice, then went on to Hendon Police College where he'd graduated at the top of his class. He had joined the Met at twenty-three; making detective at the age of twenty-six, detective sergeant before he was thirty and detective inspector by thirty-five. Now, as the head of a newly created branch of the NCA, he worked closely with the Home Office to deal what they had come to call 'Immigration Fraud'.

Maule-Ffinch greeted Carstairs warmly, shaking his hand and patting his right shoulder with his left hand in an annoyingly over-familiar way. He introduced Doctaroo and her friends and then suggesting that Carstairs take the lead, he ushered Doctaroo's party after him. They made their way along a short corridor and into a small briefing room where Carstairs indicated that they should sit.

"I don't want to keep you, so I'll make this brief," he said briskly.

He pressed a key on the laptop that lay on the table before him and a large interactive screen hanging on the wall behind, lit up. He pressed another and a picture of an Indian man in his late thirties appeared on the screen.

"This is Doctor Johar Noor. Originally from New Delhi, he arrived in this country five years ago. Background checks show that up until six months before he came to England he didn't exist."

He tapped at the laptop's keyboard again. A photograph of an auction catalogue appeared on the screen and he indicated towards several of the lots.

"Recently we were alerted to the sale of several items at Sotheby's, including a number of paintings, sculptures and various Objets d'art

34

thought to be lost to the Nazis at the end of the Second World War. The consignor, who remained anonymous, claimed to have discovered them in a barn in Provence."

Mr Walsh put up his hand. "Excuse me," he said, a look of confused boredom on his face. "But what does that have to do with this Noor person?"

Carstairs frowned at him. "I'm getting to that," he said testily.

He pressed a key on his laptop. A photograph of a golden statuette appeared on the screen. It was about fifteen inches long from tip to tail and around eight or nine inches high. Doctaroo leaned forward, squinting at the image on the screen.

"Oh, is that a cow?" she asked.

"Nah, that's a wildebeest," said Mr Walsh shaking his head.

"Technically," said Carstairs, "it's a gnu. And it once belonged to Napoleon Bonaparte. It's solid, twenty-four carat gold with 25.59 carat rubes for eyes. It sold for four point seven million pounds. Guess who bought it."

"Oooh," said Doctaroo. "I'm good at guessing. Was it Richard Branson?"

Carstairs stared at her. "No, I..."

"I know! Was it Simon Cowell?" she interrupted.

Carstairs shook his head. "No, I already told you, it was..."

"Was it The Rock?" she shouted.

"No," said Carstairs. "It wasn't The Rock, it was..."

"Well, no," Doctaroo went on. "I know he doesn't call himself that anymore, obviously I meant Dwayne Johnson."

"No! Look, Doctaroo!" Carstairs said loudly. "I meant that it was bought by Doctor Noor!"

"What, the Indian fella?" said a surprised Doctaroo.

"Yes!" Said Carstairs.

Doctaroo looked puzzled. "I thought you said he didn't exist."

Carstairs ignored her. "Noor claims to have attended MIT and has degrees in mechanical and structural engineering, particle physics and molecular biology. He holds patents on at least a dozen major scientific and ecological breakthroughs and has amassed a personal fortune rumoured to be somewhere around the four trillion mark. He is close, personal friends with several members of the cabinet, including the Prime Minister and there are whispers about knighthoods for services rendered to the Crown being bandied around."

"He sounds like a top bloke to me," said Mr Walsh.

"Aye," said Doctaroo. "He sounds like a right canny fella."

"He is. He's a great philanthropist and tireless campaigner on behalf of numerous charities around the world. He's funded dozens of wells and pipelines to bring clean, fresh water to drought-stricken parts of the Third World. He's built schools and hospitals and set up a dozen or so wildlife conservation reserves. He is genuinely adored by nations across the globe."

"So, what's the problem?" said Beryl. "If he's Mr goody-two-shoes, why are you investigatin' him?"

"Because of this." Carstairs pressed a key. An artist's impression of an astoundingly long and complex series of pipework appeared on the screen.

Doctaroo looked closely at the image. She turned her head this way and that, trying to unearth a hidden memory, a tiny hint of recognition of the pipes' shape. Finally, she clicked her fingers.

"I know what that reminds me of!" she exclaimed. "It's the London Underground!"

Carstairs nodded. "It's the Circle Line," he said grimly. "Noor bought it three years ago for a hundred and ninety million quid. He's had this pipeline laid along every mile of tunnel, connected at every station to massive state-of-the-art steam turbines. He plans to fill the pipeline with water and use geo-thermal energy from the earth's core to heat the water to boiling point, then use the steam to generate unlimited, free electricity to every home in the south east of the country."

"Then why have you got it in for him?" asked a puzzled Brian. "What's wrong with all that?"

"Well, it all seems a bit too good to be true." Maule-Ffinch said.

"It always is," sighed Doctaroo sadly. "Did I ever tell you about my Aunty Dottie?" she asked Brian and Beryl. They shook their heads. "She won the state lottery once. Ten million spondulix the prize was. Trouble was she hadn't read the fine print on the ticket. Turned out that on the planet she was on at the time, a Spondulix was a type of oily fish. A huge delicacy there of course, not so much anywhere else. Plus, they went off almost as soon as they were caught, so by the time she collected her prize, all she had were boxes and boxes of rotten fish."

"What did she do with them?" asked Beryl.

"Blended them up with some egg yolks and Worcester sauce and sold it to the locals as a health tonic. Made a fortune. Canny person, my Auntie Dot."

"So is Noor," said Carstairs. "Which is why we need your help."

He tapped at the laptop keyboard and a photograph of a familiar building appeared on the screen. "This is where Noor's company, National Utilities & Technology Services is based."

"That's an unfortunate acronym," said Doctaroo.

Mr Walsh peered at the screen. "Isn't that Canary Wharf?" he asked.

Carstairs nodded. "Yes. One Canada Square. Noor is based on the forty-seventh floor. What we need you to do, Doctaroo is to infiltrate his offices and copy the files on the hard drive of his computer onto this thumb-drive," he held up a small flash storage device, "and bring it back to us here."

Beryl laughed. "Don't be daft, soft lad," she pointed at Doctaroo. "She's no good with that sort of thing. You'd be better off asking me granny!"

Aye, pet," nodded Doctaroo. "I'd be well out of my comfort zone."

"Yeah," chipped in Mr Walsh. "You need that bloke who used to work for you during the nineties. What was his name? Henry something-or-other. Ran that troubleshooting firm."

"Henry McLachlan?" asked Maule-Ffinch. "We tried, but he's gone to ground after that unfortunate business in Baghdad a few years ago. His company, D.E.B.U.G.S went belly up shortly after. Rumour has it that he sold every share he owned to an Israeli businessman just before the stock market crash of 2016. Made a killing, apparently. However, the Israeli businessman wasn't too happy about it."

"There's a price on his head," said Carstairs. "A big one too. A lot of people have been looking for him but to no avail. He's just disappeared."

"Oh, I think I can root him out," said Doctaroo confidently.

"Well," said Carstairs taking a deep but sceptical breath, "I wish you luck. If you can find him *and* persuade him to help, then I'll buy you dinner at the Dorchester to celebrate."

"Oh, that'd be champion," said a delighted Doctaroo. "But you don't have to go to all that extravagance. Nando's will suit me just fine."

"Nonsense, Doctaroo. I insist. Besides, I can write it off as expenses." Carstairs crossed to the window and opened the blinds, looking out across the Thames at the South Bank.

"That's typical, innit?" Mr Walsh burst out angrily. "Living in luxury at the taxpayers' expense? You should be ashamed, mate." He spat the last word at Carstairs as though it left a bitter aftertaste in his mouth. Carstairs looked coldly at him and opened his mouth to offer a cutting rebuke.

There was a tinkling of broken glass and the front of Carstairs' face, from forehead to philtrum, exploded outward in a gushing fountain of scarlet. Blood, bone and brain matter burst forth and spattered over a horrified Maule-Ffinch who was standing beside the Inspector.

Chapter Four.

Without hesitation, Brian grabbed Doctaroo and Beryl and pulled them to the floor behind one of the tables. Mr Walsh and Maule-Ffinch dived for cover behind another. Carstairs' body collapsed to the floor like a marionette that had its strings cut. Doctaroo looked over at the twitching corpse of the late DCI.

"I suppose that dinner is off the cards now?" she said, sadly.

They waited behind the desks for what seemed like an age. Eventually, Maule-Ffinch raised his head above the metaphorical parapet and looked cautiously through the hole in the window. Doctaroo and the others held their breath as Maule-Ffinch stood slowly up and moved over to the shattered pane. He stood there for a good five minutes before Doctaroo, deciding that if the civil servant wasn't yet lying in a pool of his own congealed blood, then

1. there was a pretty good chance that the shooter was only targeting the DCI,

2. he or she or possibly it had packed up and left or,

3. a little from column A and a little from column B.

Banking on the latter, she got to her feet and crept cautiously over to where Maule-Ffinch was examining the window, with its cobweb-like series of cracks that emanated from the neat 50mm hole that lay in its centre.

"Blimey," she said in awe. "That was a good shot!"

Maule-Ffinch nodded. "Yes. Whoever shot Inspector Carstairs was a professional."

"Aye," agreed Doctaroo. "He'd have to be, to manage to shoot a bullet through that little hole in the window..."

After the clamour that followed Carstairs assassination had died down and the late Detective Chief Inspector's body had been taken away to the morgue, Maule-Ffinch tried to re-establish some semblance of order to the proceedings. He despatched Mr Walsh and Beryl to Canary Wharf along with the thumb-drive to attempt to steal the information they needed from Noor's computer. Meanwhile he, Brian and Doctaroo made their way, by taxi this time, to Kensington where they were greeted by a cordon around the part of Hyde Park where her Trydis had landed.

Marching briskly up to the officer in charge of the cordon, Maule-Ffinch waved his credentials at the nonplussed constable and they headed into the park to where Doctaroo had left her ship.

Walking up to the door, Doctaroo fumbled in her pockets for her keys and then opened the door. She ushered her companions in and the door slammed shut behind them.

If anybody had been walking near the vicinity of the ship, their ears would have been assaulted by a sound so indescribable that to attempt to even try to describe it here would be both pointless and unnecessary, as not only would it take up far too much of this story's running time, but it's been more than adequately explored in other books before this one.

Because of this, we politely suggest that when you've finished this, you go and read those as well.

So, with the sound that has been alluded to previously, Doctaroo's Trydis took off and showing a complete lack of respect for Sir Isaac Newton, hovered away over the rooftops of London in the general direction of the Scottish Highlands.

Doctor Johar Yashvardan Noor had been born in the Shahdara district of New Delhi in 1972. His father owned a large house near the Yamuna

River and young Johar spent his childhood playing in Chattariwala Park and hanging around the Vikas Cine Mall. His family immigrated to America in 1980, his father's job as one of India's foremost neurosurgeons having attracted the attention of the US's top private hospitals.

Making him an offer he would have been a fool to refuse, they wooed Dr Noor Snr. halfway around the world with the promise of a Hollywood practice, a three-day working week, a house in Beverley Hills and a seven-figure salary.

Johar was a shoo-in for a place at the Harvard-Westlake School, where he excelled at physics and sports. He learned to play both classical violin *and* piano and was offered a scholarship to the prestigious Juilliard School to study music. He turned it down, preferring instead to study physics at Harvard before going on to study physics and engineering at the Massachusetts Institute of Technology where he gained his PHD.

That's the official story. The one that had been anonymously uploaded to Wikipedia two years previously.

The truth, however, is both completely different and, in the context of this story, utterly irrelevant.

What *is* relevant is the tall, skinny, almost skeletal figure that had just entered a luxury penthouse suite in an exclusive hotel carrying a heavy bag that contained an AW50 sniper rifle with telescopic sight.

The man wore a plain black, three-piece suit over a white shirt and black tie. He had black closely-cropped hair and cold, pale blue eyes. He had a wide, thin mouth with harsh, cruel lips and a scar that ran from his forehead to his chin, bisecting his face and running under the steel prosthetic nose he wore in place of his real one.

Gaspard Renifler was wanted for questioning by the FBI, CIA, Interpol and MI6, to name but few. He had warrants for his arrest issued in several major countries and a good deal of minor ones too.

None of this bothered him though. His employer, who had contacts in some very, very high places, ensured that for the most part, Renifler could operate with relative impunity. He placed the bag on a glass-topped coffee table and sat down on the adjacent cream leather sofa. He unzipped the bag, removed the rifle with the kind of reverence scholars usually reserve for priceless artefacts and proceeded to clean the weapon thoroughly.

The phone rang. He answered it. A soft cultured voice spoke to him from the receiver.

"Is it done?"

Renifler smiled. "Everything went smoothly."

"I trust you weren't discovered?"

Renifler sat back on the sofa and crossed his legs. "Of course. They have no idea as to who was the shooter. It could have been her Majesty the Queen for all they know."

The voice on the phone laughed. "Excellent! Dispose of the weapon, then come and join me here."

Renifler frowned. "But M'sieur, it's an AW50.It took me weeks to find the right one."

"It's just a gun. And one that can link you to the murder of a Scotland Yard detective if it's found. Dispose of it."

Renifler was horrified. "It's not just a gun, M'sieur. It's a precision instrument, tuned to perfection. A thing of beauty which, in the right hands, can perform as exquisitely as a prima ballerina on the opening night of Swan Lake."

"It's a tool," said the voice wearily, "just like you are. Get rid of it and join me here. That's an order."

Renifler sighed sadly, "Oui, M'sieur." Replacing the receiver, Renifler stroked the gun gently.

"Au revoir, ma Cherie." He murmured regretfully and put the rifle bag into its bag. He sat for a moment, remembering how it felt in his hands. The weight of the stock against his shoulder; the coldness of the barrel; the clarity of the digital scope pressed firmly against his eye. He stood and picked up the bag, deciding to do something he never normally would ever consider. He would disobey an order. He would take the rifle and hide it, returning at a later date to collect it. He would lie to his employer; tell him that he had destroyed the weapon. Renifler felt warmth spreading throughout his nether regions. He checked that he hadn't wet himself and when he was sure that he had not, he took the rifle into the bedroom. He would have an hour alone with the gun. One hour. Surely no-one would deny him that?

Chapter Five.

Beryl and Mr. Walsh stood outside One Canada Square, the most imposing building in Canary Wharf and the second tallest building in the UK. Beryl had never seen anything like it before and she marvelled at how anything could be so huge.

"You want huge, my girl, wait until you've seen The Shard," he said gazing up at the stainless steel structure. "Now *that's* huge."

"How many people work here?" she asked. Mr Walsh shrugged.

"Dunno," he said. But this Noor fella has his offices on the forty seventh floor, so I'd reckon quite a few."

"Blimey, forty-seventh? I hope there's a lift." Beryl muttered

"You and me both, love," said Mr Walsh. He held up the duffel bag he'd been given just before the car had arrived to take them from Scotland Yard to the Docklands area of London. It had dropped them off at Cabot Square and they had walked the rest of the way.

"Our disguises are in here, apparently," he said tossing her the bag. "I hope it's something stylish like James Bond would wear."

Beryl rooted through the bag and gave a snort of derision. "Oh, yeah? You fancy yourself as Sean Connery then, do yer?"

Mr Walsh laughed. "Sean Connery's eighty nine love. I see myself as more of a Pierce Brosnan type."

"Pierced wha'?" asked Beryl.

"Not pierced, Pierce. He was the fifth proper Bond," replied Mr Walsh.

"There's five James Bonds?" squealed Beryl.

"Six actually. Soon to be seven." Mr Walsh struck a pose, pointing the fingers of his right hand like a gun.

"Yeah, I can really see myself as James Bond."

"Well, I hope you can see yerself dressed as a cleaning lady, 'cos that's what they've given us," laughed Beryl, holding up a tabard a long blonde wig and a pair of rubber gloves.

Mr. Walsh took them from her. "Oh well," he said, "there goes my dreams of being a world famous super-spy."

"Yeah, I've always wondered about that," said Beryl, taking an identical outfit out of the duffel bag. "I mean, how can he be a decent spy if *everyone* knows who he is?"

"Who?" asked Mr Walsh.

"James Bond," said Beryl. "He's always going around telling people his name and he's known in every hotel he stays at. They're always going 'Ah, Mr Bond. Your usual suite?' How he's not ever found out, I'll never know."

"Poetic license, my girl," Mr. Walsh said, putting on the tabard and the wig.

"How do I look?" He gave a twirl and Beryl laughed loudly.

"Oh my god!" she giggled. "You look like me nan!"

"Watch it!" warned Mr. Walsh, which set Beryl off into another fit of giggles.

"Come over here," she said, crossing over to a nearby bench. "Sit down and I'll make you look more presentable."

Mr. Walsh sat down beside her and she took her make-up bag from her handbag.

"How do you feel about false eyelashes? Beryl asked, rooting in her make-up bag. She pulled out her compact and lipstick and put them on the bench next to her.

"This is my spare set, the ones I use when I'm going out on the razz with the girls."

Mr. Walsh leaned forward so that Beryl could stick on the eyelashes. She then powdered his cheeks, nose, and applied the lipstick. When she had finished, she sat back to admire her creation.

"Now you really *do* look like me nan," she said with a grin. She removed a mirror from the bag and showed Mr. Walsh his reflection.

"Phoar," he said, pouting at the person in the mirror. "Not bad at all. I could quite go for myself."

Beryl frowned at him. "D'you know I'm not sure if I'm more creeped out by that or how comfortable you are all dolled up like a barmaid from Bootle. If I didn't know better, I'd swear you've done this before."

"East Bromley Amateur Dramatics Society treasurer, 1997 to 2012. My Desdemona got rave reviews in the Bromley and District Times," said Mr. Walsh getting to his feet and dancing around in a circle in front of Beryl. She laughed and applauded his antics.

"Bravo, bravo!" she shouted, "encore!"

Mr. Walsh stopped dancing as he noticed that he was attracting attention from a small group of office workers who had popped out for a crafty cigarette. Quickly grabbing Beryl by the hand, he pulled her over to where several women wearing similar protective garments as them, were entering the building through a side door. Keeping their heads down, they mingled unobtrusively with the group as they made their way across the foyer and through a door marked 'Staff Only'.

Inside, they followed the women to a locker room where they stashed the duffel bag inside an empty locker, then they joined a couple of women who headed to the staff canteen. Once there, they split off from the pair and found a corner where they could sit and plan their next move.

On the forty seventh floor, Johar Noor was putting the finishing touches to the speech he was to give at the party that would mark the grand 'unveiling' and switching -on of his greatest accomplishment.

It was going to be an evening of huge surprises, he thought as he typed out the final paragraph on his computer. Getting the Queen to actually perform the switch-on was a coup in itself and he'd had to call in rather more favours than he'd hoped in order to ensure that the party would go off with a royal 'bang', so to speak. But, he supposed, if things go the way his benefactor assured him they would go, then it will have all been worth the effort. He suppressed a giggle, wondering whether he could persuade Her Majesty to wear one of his company's baseball caps when she pressed the switch.

He finished the speech and sat back in his chair with a satisfied sigh. He reached out to the bottle of expensive craft beer he had earlier taken from the fridge and took a long swig. His mobile rang. He checked the screen to see who it was. No caller ID. He answered it.

"Johar, my dear fellow, how are you?" purred a silky male voice from the receiver. "I trust everything is proceeding exactly as we designed it?"

Noor took another swig from the beer bottle and swallowed loudly. "Of course," he said after a moment. "Did you doubt it?"

"Not at all," came the reply, a slight trace of amusement in his voice. "This is just a courtesy call. I don't mean to imply that I'm checking up on you."

"And yet," said Noor coldly, "here you are doing it anyway."

The voice changed in tone, a flinty hardness creeping into it. A voice that brooked no argument. A voice that most definitely implied that, even if it cracked a joke, it was still not to be trifled with. Noor decided not to trifle with it.

"Please be assured, my dear Doctor, that you are most certainly not irreplaceable," the voice said icily.

"I'm sorry, sir," said Noor quickly. "Everything is in order, you have my word."

There was a pause from the other end of the line. Then, "Very well. But just in case we're still not on the same page, I'll be sending a couple of our, ah, *colleagues* to keep a watchful eye on the proceedings."

"That's really not necess..." began Noor. The voice interrupted sharply.

"Nevertheless, it would put my mind at rest to know that everything is in order."

"It is, believe me," stammered Noor.

"No," the voice said coldly, "you believe me. If the collider isn't activated on the Nineteenth as per our arrangement, then you have my assurance that you will regret ever having met me. Is that clear?"

Noor licked dry lips. "Crystal clear sir. You have *my* assurance that it will be ready *ahead* of schedule."

"Good," replied the voice. "Make sure of it." The phone clicked off.

Noor drained the bottle. There was, he thought wryly, not the tiniest shadow of a doubt that he already regretted ever having met his mysterious benefactor.

Not. One. Doubt.

Chapter Six.

Doctaroo landed her Trydis near a small drystone Croft situated somewhere between Fort William and Mallaig on the west coast of the Scottish Highlands.

Well, *landed* isn't really the most apposite way to describe the twitchy, twirly, bumpy, crashy way it came to rest amid the heather and bracken. That word, if given voice, would be best described as, "*Aaarrgh!!!*"

The door slid open. First Doctaroo, wearing a yellow cagoule, thick jumper, trousers and wellington boots, exited the phone box, then Brian and Maule-Ffinch followed cautiously out. Both Brian and Maule-Finch wore similar outfits to Doctaroo,

Outside the Croft stood two burly men in Highland dress. Both armed with Glock 17s even though, judging by how they looked, neither of them would ever feel the need to use them. Rippling muscles bulged under tight, white T-shirts, while their legs, each the thickness of the cabers they were probably proficient in tossing, poked out from beneath their kilts. Doctaroo gave a squeal and ran over to them.

"Ooh, I *love* a man in a kilt!" she yelled.

The nearest man pulled his Glock from its holster and pointed it at her. His colleague did the same.

"Stand where ye are!" he shouted. Doctaroo stopped dead in her tracks.

"Oh, Howay pet," she called cheerily. "It's me, Doctaroo."

The man lowered his weapon slowly. "The Doctaroo?" he asked. "Lulu's nightclub in Edinburgh, Doctaroo?"

"The very same," she said giving him a twirl. "How are you Hamish?" she giggled.

Hamish gave her a cheerful grin. "Och aye, well enough. Hey Dougal," he called to his friend. "It's Doctaroo, frae Lulu's in Edinburgh."

"Aye, right enough," replied Dougal. "Is it yourself, Doctaroo?"

Doctaroo gave them both a hug. "Is Henry at home?" she asked once she had extricated herself from their clutches. Hamish nodded.

"Aye, he's inside playing with his equipment," he said with a roguish grin. Doctaroo squealed with delight.

"Ooh, I'd best not disturb him then!" she giggled.

Maule-Ffinch and Brian approached them cautiously. Dougal pointed a thumb in their direction.

"Who're your pals?" he asked with a growl. Maule-Ffinch winced and unconsciously moved an inch closer to Brian.

"Oh, they're just groupies, you know?" she smiled coquettishly up at the big Scot. "They're always hanging around, they're harmless. Can we go in and see Henry?"

Dougal shrugged and looked at Hamish for confirmation. Hamish nodded so Dougal moved to open the door.

"I should warn you," he said, "he's been a wee bit paranoid recently. Keeps talking about giant lizards or something coming to get him in the night."

"It's no' lizards, Dougal," corrected Hamish. "It's aardvarks or anteaters or something. If you ask me," he whispered conspiratorially to Doctaroo, "I think he's a wee bit aff his heid."

"Aww, bless him," said Doctaroo gently. "It happens to the best of us. I think I went a bit potty a few bodies ago, but I'm better now. A new face is as good as a nice holiday sometimes."

Dougal turned the key and pushed open the door to the Croft. Doctaroo strolled merrily in,

64

followed cautiously by Brian and Maule-Ffinch. Dougal decided to give the obviously frightened civil servant a very hard stare as he passed by, causing Maule-Ffinch to cower back in fear. Hamish, buoyed on by his friend's glare, thought he would join in with a growl. Both men moved closer together, sandwiching the terrified man between them, which caused Maule-Ffinch to run into the Croft, barging past Brian and only coming to a halt when he saw the technological impossibility that was its interior.

Banks of 1970s computers lined one wall; magnetic tape machines spooled and whirred along another. It was like stepping back in time into an episode of Tomorrow's World.

Sitting in an office chair in the centre of all of this and staring at a bank of CRT monitors was a moderately handsome, well-built blonde man of about thirty years of age. However, Maule-Ffinch knew that looks could be deceiving if Doctaroo was anything to go by.

The man looked up in surprise as they entered. He stared at them for a second, and then a look of recognition crossed his face on seeing Doctaroo's cheerful expression. Just as quickly, one of anger replaced that look and he jumped to his feet, his chair shooting backwards and into one of the tape machines.

"How the bloody hell did you find me?" he demanded, in an antipodean twang. "I thought I'd covered my tracks!"

"Aww, bless you pet," said Doctaroo.

Maule-Ffinch stepped forward. "Mister Henry McLachlan?" he asked. "My name is Nigel Maule-Ffinch from the Home Office."

Henry McLachlan's eyes widened and his face reddened with rage. He glared at Doctaroo.

"You've brought one of *them* with you? Do you realise what this means? Do you?" he demanded, stepping closer and looming menacingly over Nigel.

Doctaroo just shrugged. Maule-Ffinch shrank away and cleared his throat nervously.

"Ahem, what does it mean, Mr. McLachlan?" he asked, his voice trembling.

Henry looked at him coldly.

66

"It means," he said, slowly and deliberately. "That I'll have to send out for a fresh bottle of milk, unless you prefer your coffee black."

He suddenly burst into peals of raucous laughter.

"Oh, the look on your face!" he chuckled. He called out to his two bodyguards.

"Hamish! Dougal! Come in here and have a look at this drongo!"

The two Scots came in to have a laugh at the embarrassed Maule-Ffinch who stared fixedly at a spot he had found on the floor. Henry reached forward and clapped the miserable civil servant on the shoulder.

"Aww, fair dinkum, mate. I saw what was going on outside on my monitor over there," he indicated his bank of screens. "I couldn't resist."

Maule-Ffinch shuffled uncomfortably. Doctaroo put her arm around him reassuringly.

"Poor love," she said trying unsuccessfully to hide her smile. "Howay, Henry man. That's a cruel thing to do."

"Yeah?" said McLachlan. "Then why are you grinning like a Cheshire cat?"

Brian had wandered over to the bank of computers and was examining them, a look of awe and wonder on his face.

"Blimey," he said, his eyes wide. "It's like the microchip revolution never happened!"

Henry joined him. "Awesome, isn't it? I've piggybacked my system onto half a dozen servers through a dozen VPNs at the same time in two dozen countries which means that I'm completely invisible and untraceable."

"Hang on," said Brian. "That isn't possible. Not with this antiquated junk. You'd be lucky to get dial up."

"Oh come on mate," drawled Henry. "You travel with *her*, don't you?" Brian nodded. Henry went on. "Then you should be used to the impossible."

He reached out and flicked one of the switches on a nearby computer. With a hiss, the entire front of it swung open on a hinge and Brian found himself looking at a large glowing sphere, about the size of a football, with a myriad of what appeared to be fibre optic cables intersecting with it and twisting in and out of each other and through the other computers. The occasional flashes of what seemed to be either light or electricity would pulse along the transparent cables, forward and backwards and sometimes meeting in the middle.

Brian asked what it was. Henry leaned closer and whispered in his ear.

"Those are thoughts mate," he said, his voice like honey. "Pure thoughts."

"But… how?" asked Brian. Henry smiled and tapped his nose. The computer closed with another hiss. Doctaroo frowned at Henry.

"You're a bad lad, Henry McLachlan. You know you're not supposed to have access to alien tech. That's what you agreed to last time we met."

Henry shrugged. "So, sue me."

Maule-Ffinch interrupted them excitedly. "But this is perfect," he said happily. "You can look into Dr. Noor without the fear of being discovered."

Henry looked blankly at him. Doctaroo decided to explain.

Chapter Seven.

Beryl and Mr Walsh poked their heads around a corner. There was no one in sight, so Mr Walsh nudged her sharply in the ribs.

"Over there," he said, pointing at a row of lifts.

They ran over and pushed the call button. Mr Walsh looked around furtively. Suddenly he darted off to one side leaving Beryl to anxiously wait for the lift to arrive. When Mr Walsh returned he was pushing a mop bucket in front of him and carrying a couple of mops under one arm.

"Well, we *are* supposed to be cleaners after all, ain't we? These'll help us maintain our cover."

The lift door opened with a ping and the pair all but fell inside, each carrying a mop and with Beryl kicking the bucket across the lift's floor. The doors closed behind them.

"There," said Mr Walsh. "Hit number forty-seven."

Beryl pressed the button and the lift whooshed upwards at speed. Pretty soon they arrived at the forty-seventh floor, Mr Walsh offering a silent prayer to whoever the patron saint of secret agents was that they hadn't had to stop at any other floor to pick up new passengers. He had started to feel conspicuous in his disguise and had begun to doubt whether his wig and make-up would, in truth, fool anyone. Perhaps, he thought to himself, the false eyelashes were a step too far. But then he did think he looked good in them, so maybe...

He was brought back to reality by Beryl dragging him out of the lift. The offices of National Utilities, Transport & Shipping, was an open-plan affair. The rooms were set out like the board of a

71

Trivial Pursuit game, with a reception desk at the centre. Each office was made from a different material, one was wood-panelled, one was steel, etc.

You get the drift.

"Hey, steady on," gasped Mr Walsh. "I'm a lady."

"Yeah? Pay attention then, your ladyship. We're here and we've a job to do." Beryl was pointing to a frosted-glass walled office. The nameplate on the door read: Dr Johar Noor. CEO.

Mr Walsh pretended to mop the floor, gradually moving closer. As he got near, he reached out to surreptitiously turn the handle. It didn't budge.

"It's locked," he whispered. Beryl frowned.

"Hang on, I've got an idea." She handed him her mop and strode confidently up to the reception desk, where a pretty blonde-haired receptionist was mid-conversation with someone who, by the way the conversation was going, could only be her other half. Beryl tapped impatiently on the glass desk.

The receptionist put her hand over the mouthpiece of the phone.

"Yes?" she said, sharply. Beryl gave the girl her most dazzling smile.

"Oh, hiya luv," she said, giving her best Margi Clarke impression. "Me and me friend, er, Doris over there," she pointed at Mr Walsh, who had suddenly started to pretend that he was polishing the glass wall of Dr Noor's office.

Beryl continued. "Well we've hit a bit of a snag. We're supposed to clean Dr Noor's office, but the door's locked and Doris," she indicated Mr Walsh again who gave a cheery wave, "has forgotten her pass key, the dozy mare. I don't suppose you've gorra spare, have yer?"

The receptionist frowned and explained as frostily as she could that she couldn't give out the key to all and sundry. Beryl gave her another million dollar smile.

"Well that's perfectly understandable, luv. But I'd hate to be the one to explain to Dr Noor why his bin hadn't been emptied or his awards polished."

She knew she was grasping at straws, but she didn't have that much to work with and she was banking on

A. The receptionist not being interested in security that much,

B. The receptionist wanting to get back to her conversation with her fella and

C. The receptionist being sufficiently concerned with what her employer would say if, indeed, his awards hadn't been polished.

It turned out that Beryl was correct on all three points and the girl behind the desk opened a draw and handed her a key on a brightly coloured key-ring.

"I want that back when you're finished," she warned as Beryl walked back to her friend.

Beryl gave her the thumbs up and unlocked the door to Noor's office. She followed Mr Walsh in and shut the door after them. Mr Walsh ran around the heavy oak desk that occupied the far side of the room, away from the door. Behind it was a floor to ceiling window that offered a superb view of London.

74

On the walls were a series of prints by Kandinsky. At least Mr Walsh assumed them to be prints. Given Dr Noor's proclivity for buying valuable antiquities at auction, they could well be original pieces. In which case, he made a mental note to alert the fraud squad, or whoever it was that dealt with art theft as soon as they got back.

The only other piece of furniture in the room was a full length, free standing mirror. Beryl checked her appearance while Mr Walsh took out the thumb drive given to him earlier by Maule-Ffinch. He plugged it into a spare USB port and wiggled the mouse to wake up the PC. The security screen lit up and Mr Walsh frowned.

"Bugger," he said. "It's password protected."

"How many characters?" asked Beryl, pouting at her reflection.

"Six," said Mr Walsh.

"Well, try 123456," replied Beryl re-applying her lipstick. Mr Walsh gave her a withering look.

"Seriously? Who in their right mind would use that as their password?" he said tapping at the keyboard.

"Oh, I'm in."

"See," said Beryl applying mascara. "I'm not just a pretty face y'know."

Mr Walsh grinned. "I take it all back, girl." He dragged the relevant files over to the thumb-drive's open folder on the desktop. "This might take a while, there's a lot to copy across."

Beryl leaned against the desk. She looked around casually. "How come there's no chairs in here?"

"Dunno," said Mr Walsh wandering over to inspect one of the prints. "Perhaps he's not one for sitting down. Or maybe he doesn't use his office much." He licked a finger and rubbed at a corner of the picture. The ink came off on it.

"Hang on," he said. "That shouldn't have happened." He took out a tissue from his tabard and wet it in the mop bucket, then wiped the centre of the picture. The ink smeared.

Beryl got up to have a look. "That's weird," she said.

"You're telling me. Why put up a newly printed picture?"

Beryl shrugged. "Maybe he's only just got it," she suggested. Mr Walsh shook his head.

"Even so," he said, rubbing at the next picture along. The ink came off on that one too. "There's something odd going on here." He lifted the print from the wall. Behind it lay a small recess containing a lens.

"Bugger," he said. "We're being watched."

There was a chime from the computer and Beryl checked the screen. The files had finished transferring over to the thumb-drive. Mr Walsh joined her, ejected the drive and shut down the computer.

"Come on," he said and headed for the door. Beryl started to follow, then stopped dead in her tracks. She screamed and Mr Walsh spun around to see what all the fuss was about.

The tall mirror's reflective surface had turned opaque and had then started to glow with an unearthly blue light. The glow increased in intensity causing Beryl and Mr Walsh to cover their eyes.

A tall, muscular figure began to materialise, slowly forming as though made from the very light itself. Another began to form next to it and yet another on the other side of the first.

Mr Walsh squinted at the figure, trying to define its shape through the intense incandescence emanating from the mirror. The light began to fade and blinking rapidly in an attempt to readjust his eyes, Mr Walsh tried to focus on the beings that had materialised from the mirror.

The creatures were tall, at least two metres high, dressed in armour that resembled that of an ancient Roman gladiator. Their arms and legs were naked, save for a short kilt-like garment it wore around its waist and what looked to be leather cuffs, decorated with silver studs on their wrists. They carried long spear-like sharp edged weapons and had blasters tucked into holsters attached to their belts.

On their heads they wore ornate bejewelled helmets, with ruby red eye slits and brightly coloured crests that ran from the top of the head down to the nape of the neck.

The lead creature raised its hands to its head and removed its helmet. For the first time, Mr Walsh and Beryl were able to get a good look at the face of the newcomer.

It was almost reptilian in appearance, although the downy hair that covered its skin belied its mammalian origins. A series of hard plates ran from its forehead, down the back of its neck and beneath its armour.

What looked to be heavy plated pauldrons covered its shoulders and joined with similar plates that covered its back.

Two red eyes sat in deeply lined sockets and when it opened its mouth to smile at them, Beryl could make out dozens of sharp little teeth that it ran its tongue across, lasciviously.

The Kkrellem had arrived.

Chapter Eight.

Doctaroo finally persuaded Henry to go with them back to Scotland Yard where she hoped Beryl and Mr Walsh would have the files from Noor's computer. Working on the assumption that they would be encrypted, Henry started work on an algorithm that would, in theory, be able to decipher any encrypted file fed into it.

In less time that it takes to microwave a frozen lasagne, Doctaroo's Trydis had taken them from Scotland to London and she parked it neatly (which was a miracle, according to Brian) on top of the Curtis Green building. They made their way down to the late DCI Carstairs' office and were greeted by his hastily appointed replacement.

DCI Cedric Carstairs.

Doctaroo stared at him open mouthed as did both Brian and Maule-Ffinch. Henry, who hadn't known of the Inspector's demise greeted him with a cheery, "G'day!"

Carstairs smiled warmly. "How do you do. Mr McLachlan, isn't it?"

"Nah, only me teachers and me parole officer call me Mr McLachlan. I'm Henry to me pals," said Henry with a huge grin.

Doctaroo sat down on the sofa that sat against opposite Carstairs' desk. She continued to stare at the DCI. Brian shrugged and sat next to her, while a visibly shaken Maule-Ffinch poured himself a large whisky from the decanter on Carstairs' sideboard.

"How the f…" began Doctaroo, before remembering that this is supposed to be a children's book, despite the graphic violence. She stopped and tried again. "How the bloomin' heck are you still alive?" she asked incredulously. "I saw your head explode!"

Carstairs sat down behind his desk. "Heh, heh. Reports of my death have been greatly exaggerated," he said quoting an infinitely better author than I.

"Allow me to introduce the Met's latest weapon in the fight against crime." He held up a black box of about the same size and shape of a mobile phone. Doctaroo leaned forward.

"Oooh," she said. "What's that?"

"It's my mobile phone," Carstairs replied.

"That's not much of a weapon," said Doctaroo with a sniff. "Not unless you're going to use it to call for help."

"No," began Carstairs, "the phone's not the weapon…" He rubbed a hand over his eyes and pinched the bridge of his nose with his thumb and forefinger.

"Look, I'll just show you shall I?" he said wearily. He touched the phone's screen and a panel in the wall to the left of his desk slid up. Behind it stood another DCI Carstairs. Carstairs got up and crossed over to stand by his doppelganger.

"This is ME2," he said smiling at his double. "Hello, ME2."

The copy smiled back. "Hello Detective Chief Inspector," it replied in the same voice.

Carstairs turned back to the others. "ME2 is the latest in our Science Division's experiments in genetic duplication," he said. "He's perfect down to every detail."

Henry crossed the room to examine ME2. "You mean he's a clone?" he whispered. "How fascinating."

Carstairs shook his head. "ME2 isn't just a clone, Henry. He's a living, breathing artificial organism. He's been programmed with my memories, mannerisms and inordinately good looks!"

Henry tilted his head. "An android then?"

ME2 smiled at him and then turned to Carstairs. "If I may, Detective Chief Inspector?" Carstairs nodded. ME2 turned back to Henry. "I am a genetically engineered artificial lifeform. A *biological* android if you prefer."

Doctaroo put up her hand. "I'm confused," she said.

Carstairs rolled his eyes. "Why doesn't that surprise me," he muttered under his breath. Then, aloud: "Go on, Doctaroo. What's confusing you?"

Doctaroo shifted uncomfortably on the sofa. "Well, why the heck you bought this sofa for a kick off. It's like sitting bare-bum on a bucket full of gravel." She got up and adjusting her pants, waddled over to ME2.

"So, who got shot then? 'Cos this fella looks brand new." She prodded him on the nose. ME2 looked benignly back at her.

"That was ME1," said Carstairs.

"Mel?" asked Doctaroo.

"No." Carstairs said patiently. "ME1. It just looks like Mel when you write it down, it's pronounced Me One."

"Oh," said Doctaroo happily. "I just wanted to check like. In case it confused the readers."

"So, they're like decoys then?" asked Brian.

Carstairs nodded. "Yes. I suppose you could say that. We'd had word from MI6 that Gaspard Renifler had been sighted coming into the country at Gatwick Airport."

"Oh, aye," said Doctaroo. "Who's this Gassy Jennifer when she's at home?"

"*Gaspard Renifler* is an international terrorist and political assassin," said ME2. "He is wanted by the security services of at least eleven countries and has over a dozen outstanding warrants worldwide for his arrest. Renifler is a nickname earned due to the prosthetic nose he now wears after his own was bitten off by a rabid Chihuahua in Cartagena, in 1982. His real name is unknown." ME2 turned to Carstairs. "Do you have any further use of my services Detective Chief Inspector?"

Carstairs shook his head. "No thank you ME2. I'll call you if I need you."

"Very well, Detective Chief Inspector. I will be in the laboratory should you require further assistance." ME2 stepped down from the alcove and nodding to Doctaroo and the others, walked calmly and unhurriedly from the room.

"I had a tip off that my life might be in danger," explained Carstairs.

"So I activated ME1 and had him stand in for me at the briefing this morning. I'm sorry if it shocked you, but we had to make it look real in case our Intel was correct."

Doctaroo shook her head in awe. She nudged Brian. "The mind boggles, doesn't it Brian? I mean it seems so fantastic I can hardly believe it. It's like something out of a comic book." Carstairs nodded in agreement.

"Indeed, Doctaroo. In fact that's where we got the idea for our Artificial Intelligence Decoy and Escort system - that's what we're calling them by the way, Artificial Intelligence Decoy and Escorts or AIDEs. We're having some grown at the moment as stand-ins for the Royal Family," he grinned cheerfully. "It really is all rather exciting. We're at the forefront of some really cutting-edge technology."

Maule-Ffinch poured himself another whisky. "I'd be very interested to know why my office hadn't been informed of any of this, Cedric," he asked haughtily.

Carstairs looked suitably apologetic. "Need to know, Nigel. The Home Secretary has been appraised of the situation. If he didn't see fit to inform you then I'm certain he had his reasons. National security and all that, you know."

Maule-Ffinch looked hurt. "Well, it would have been nice to have been told, Cedric, that's all. Now I'll have to go and cancel the wreath I'd ordered for your funeral."

Mr Walsh and Beryl sat back to back on the floor of Noor's office while the Kkrellem leader spoke to someone with a soft, silky voice on the other end of its communicator. For such a fearsome looking creature, the Kkrellem had an unusually gentle voice and Mr Walsh strained to listen in on its conversation with its mysterious contact.

"What should we do with the human creatures?" it queried.

"Nothing. Keep them there until I arrive," said the voice.

"Kkrank would like permission to eat one of them," it asked. "The female looks especially flavoursome," it drooled.

"Tell Kkrank to stay well away from them. I want them alive. Do you understand that, Kkrask?"

"What of the other female?" Kkrask asked. "The painted one outside the room."

"Do you mean my secretary, Miss Mason?" the voice said.

Kkrask growled. "Yes. The one with red claws and very little clothing."

There was a pause from the other end, then the voice sighed. "Oh, very well," it said resignedly. "But tell him to be careful. I don't want to have to clear up his table leavings when I arrive."

"He will be pleased. I will ensure that he leaves no trace." The communicator clicked off.

Kkrask gave Beryl a sharp-toothed grin and licked its lips. "Think yourself lucky, human creatures. Our master wishes us to keep you alive."

"Oh, yeah," said Mr Walsh cheerily. "I said to Beryl only this morning what lucky people we are. Didn't I Beryl?"

"You're not really gonna eat that poor girl are yer?" Beryl asked. The Kkrellem tilted its head to one side.

"Why do you care?" it asked. "Is she of value to you?"

"Well of course she's of value!" exploded Mr Walsh. "She's a human being!"

One of the other Kkrellem came over. It spoke to Kkrask in a guttural vocalisation, part animalistic growl and part sing-song chirping sounds. Kkrask replied in the same language, then turned back to his captives. He crouched down so he could look Mr Walsh straight in the eye.

"Human meat is highly prized in the markets of our world. But we have always been taught that you are a simple species with little intelligence and no provision for empathy with other members of its own kind. Yet you appear to be concerned for the life of another. Why is this?"

Mr Walsh glared back at him. "If we're supposed to be unintelligent, why are you the one asking such a stupid question?" He turned away, unwilling to discuss the matter further.

Kkrask stood up. Across the room, the Kkrellem named Kkrank was sitting cross-legged on the desk, happily sharpening a huge knife that he had taken from a sheath fastened to his belt. Kkrask walked over to him.

"Put away your blade." Kkrask said. Kkrank looked sharply at him.

"But our employer gave permission to feast on the human cow outside. I was planning to barbecue it. I'd prepared a delicious piquant sauce in which to marinate its haunches."

"I have decided to not allow it." Kkrask said firmly. "I do not believe that they are as simple as our educators have portrayed them."

Kkrank gave a short, harsh snort of derision. "I have warned you in the past about discourse with food. It never ends well."

"The older human has shown concern for its own kind, something the educators told us wasn't possible. I have no explanation for this," mused Kkrask.

"Ha! You'll be eating leaves and roots next like a deviant Kkrollum," laughed Kkrank. "Cows are bred for food, nothing else."

"I do not believe these humans *are* cows," said Kkrask. "For one thing, they are more intelligent than the humans of our world."

"*All* humans are cows!" replied Kkrank. "And we are *meant* to consume them. That is how it was written."

"But what if the writings are *wrong*?" insisted Kkrask. Kkrank jumped to his feet in alarm.

"Be quiet!" he said in a low voice. "Do not let Kkrogh hear your blasphemous words! I will overlook them because you are my elder sibling, but Kkrogh is less inclined to tolerate your eccentricities."

Kkrask glanced over at the other Kkrellem who was standing guard at the door. "Do you think he heard?" he whispered, a look of concern on his muzzle. Kkrogh's ears twitched.

Kkrank sighed. "It may be necessary to despatch Kkrogh to one of the outer worlds on a mission of misery," he said.

"Misery?" asked Kkrask. Kkrank grinned.

"Indeed. You may need to put him out of yours," he laughed.

Kkrask smiled. "Continue honing you're blade, brother," he said softly. "I will find you something suitable on which to use it."

Kkrank nodded and put his hand on Kkrask's shoulder. "Perhaps you should ask your new human friend?" he said with a chuckle.

Kkrask narrowed his eyes. "Perhaps I should have eaten you when we were in our mother's belly!" he growled.

Mr Walsh and Beryl were watching their captors closely. Mr Walsh had managed to loosen the ropes that the Kkrellem had used to tie their hands together. He pulled one hand free, then the other. A few seconds later they were both free of their bonds. He looked over at the Kkrellem guarding the door.

"How fast do you reckon those things are?" he whispered to Beryl.

"I don't know," she whispered back. "Do I look like David bleedin' Attenborough?"

He glared at her. "What I meant was, how fast are Armadillos usually? In the wild, I mean. On this planet?"

"D'yer reckon that's what they are then? Big armadillos?" Beryl asked.

Mr Walsh shrugged. "Well, they look like armadillos, don't they? *Really* big armadillos."

"I suppose so," said Beryl. "Now you come to mention it. If armadillos went around carrying big spears and ray guns and threatenin' to eat people, then they're the spit of them."

"What we need," said Mr Walsh looking around, "is a distraction."

"Yeah?" said Beryl sarcastically. "Worrave yer got in mind then, Einstein? A fan dance? Or are yer gonna give them a couple of verses of Let It Be?"

"Actually, I was thinking more like something by The Alarm," he grinned, indicating the wall above her.

She looked up, then back at Mr Walsh, a sly smile slowly spreading across her face. "Nice one Mr W," she said. "On the count of three?"

Mr Walsh nodded. "One," he said.

"Two," said Beryl.

"Three!" They both yelled as loudly as they could, before Beryl jumped to her feet and used her elbow to break the glass on the fire alarm.

Immediately, the room erupted in pandemonium. The three Kkrellem flailed wildly around, covering their ears to protect against the noise from the siren. Staggering about in obvious distress, Kkrask activated the teleportal they had arrived via and once it had fully formed, they each jumped through it. Meanwhile, in the confusion, Beryl and Mr Walsh dived for the door.

Outside, people were making for the fire exits. Beryl and Mr Walsh joined a small group who were headed for the stairwell. Beryl was divesting herself of the tabard while Mr Walsh did likewise,

94

also removing his wig at the same time. Neither of them looked back, preferring instead to concentrate on getting out of the building as quickly as possible.

After making their way down the hundreds of steps from the 47th floor, they ran as fast as they could out of the building and across the plaza to where their car was waiting to take them back to Scotland Yard. Once they were safely inside the relative comfort of the Range Rover, they allowed themselves to relax a little. Beryl let out a huge sigh of relief.

"Flippin' 'eck, Mr W. That was a stroke of genius that was. How did you know it would have such an effect on them?"

Mr Walsh panted, trying to catch his breath. "It was the armadillo thing you said," he explained. "I read somewhere that armadillos have superb senses of smell and hearing to make up for their relatively poor eyesight. It was just pure luck that those guys were similar in that way to the armadillos of our planet."

"Did you hear what they were saying though? About eatin' people? Cows they called us.

Mind you though," Beryl conceded, "I've been called a lot worse."

"Yeah, that's a bit different to real armadillos. They're still carnivores, but they eat mostly insects."

"You're dead clever you are," said Beryl. "It must be all those books in the library you used to work at."

"Well, I do pride myself on my general knowledge," he replied. "That's why I did so well on Fifteen to One and Going for Gold."

"You should go on Mastermind," said Beryl. "You'd be dead good on that."

"Oh yeah," replied Mr Walsh. "That's the one to aim for, Beryl. That's the big one." He removed the thumb drive from his shirt pocket. "I just hope that this little thing is worth all the effort it took to get it."

Chapter Nine.

Dr Noor surveyed the damage the Kkrellem had done to his office. His secretary, who to his surprise was still around, was deeply apologetic as she explained about the two cleaners she had let into the room. Noor waved her entreaties away with a beatific smile.

"Please do not concern yourself, Miss Mason," he told her. "There is nothing broken that cannot be replaced."

"But it's my fault, Dr Noor. They said they were cleaners. They had tabards on and everything."

Noor raised an eyebrow. "Indeed," he said. "The identifying power of the commercial tabard. And so, naturally, you gave them the key."

Miss Mason hung her head in shame. "I'll clear out my desk sir."

Noor shook his head. "Nonsense. You'll do no such thing. What's done is done and there is no point attempting to second guess yourself. Return to work."

Miss Mason gave him a smile of relief and went back to her desk. Noor closed the office door. He crossed to his desk and booted up his computer. He clicked the mouse several times until he found what he wanted: the feed from his security cameras.

With a frown he scrolled through the footage. "Now who are you?" he murmured. "And who do you work for..."

He took his mobile from his pocket and dialled a number. "It's me," he said. "We have a problem."

Doctaroo was picking her teeth with a nail file after polishing off a bacon double cheeseburger, very large fries, a triple chocolate milkshake and a plateful of chocolate brownies. She belched loudly.

"Oooh that one had lumps in it!" She grinned at Brian who was finishing off his burger. "Feeling better now, pet?" she asked. Brian nodded, his mouth full of beef and bacon.

They were sitting in the canteen waiting for Beryl and Mr Walsh to arrive. Brian had already eaten two double quarter pounders with cheese, three large fries and a litre of cola and as he popped the last morsel of his third burger into his mouth and with a pound and a half of premium ground steak in his belly, he pushed back his plate with a satisfied sigh.

"That was good," he said, hiccoughing slightly. "I fancy a chocolate bar. Do you fancy a chocolate bar?" he asked Doctaroo.

She shook her head. "Nah pet, I fancy that bloke off the news. Can you get him for me?"

Brian stood up. "Are you sure I can't get you anything from the machine?"

"If you fancy running down to Starbucks," she suggested, "I'd love a tall black Americano. Or failing that I'll have a coffee!"

She burst into a fit of giggles again. Brian noted that she often did that when she was worried about something. The crap jokes usually covered up some anxiety or other too. The constant sexual harassment of pretty much any conscious, or even semi-conscious male However, was just something she enjoyed.

"Sure," he said holding out his hand. "I need some cash though."

"Typical," said Doctaroo rummaging in her left hand trouser pocket. She pulled out a handful of banknotes. "Here you go, pet, I'm sure there's something you can use in that lot."

Brian pocketed the money and left the canteen.

Doctaroo wrinkled her nose. "You could have waited until you got outside before you farted!" she shouted after him. "Dirty bugger," she muttered under her breath and tried to waft away the smell with a copy of Metro she found on a chair. The canteen door opened and Carstairs walked in, deep in conversation with Maule-Ffinch. They reached Doctaroo's table and Maule-Ffinch put his hand over his nose.

"Ugh," he said in distaste. "What on Earth is that smell?"

"Brian," replied Doctaroo. "And three double quarter-pounders. He's gone for coffee, you've just missed him."

"Never mind that," said Carstairs, sitting down opposite. "I've just had word from my contact at Canary Wharf that there's been a bit of a commotion on the forty seventh floor."

"Ooh, that's a coincidence," said Doctaroo. "That Noor fella works there. Beryl and Mr Walsh have gone there to spy on him."

Carstairs looked blankly at her, then gave Maule-Ffinch a look that seemed to semaphore the word HELP in big red letters. He cleared his throat and sat down next to Doctaroo.

"Yes, Doctaroo. We assume the commotion was caused by them. Their driver has already radioed in and they'll be here soon."

"Ohhh, champion. Then you'll be able to ask them if they saw the commotion you were on about."

Carstairs opened the file he had been carrying and showed her a couple of blurred photographs. Obviously taken with a long lens from an adjacent building, one showed Mr Walsh at Noor's computer. The other showed what looked like an anthropomorphic, six foot armadillo wearing armour. Doctaroo picked up the picture and studied it carefully. Carstairs leaned forward.

"Do you recognise that creature?" he asked. Doctaroo shook her head.

"It looks a bit like my Uncle Frank," she said. "Only it hasn't got a beard and a beer belly. And my Uncle Frank doesn't wear armour. And he isn't an armadillo. Other than that it's the spittin' image of him."

Carstairs opened his mouth to speak, but was interrupted by the door bursting open and Beryl

102

and Mr Walsh ran in breathlessly. They fell into a couple of chairs and drank greedily from the glasses of water a constable brought them. Doctaroo tried to suppress a smile and failed utterly.

"Eee, that lipstick really suits you, Mr Walsh," she said with a chuckle. "And that eyeshadow really brings out your eyes."

Mr Walsh smiled back. "Oh do you think so?" He asked. "I've always thought aquamarine was my colour..."

"Do you have the thumb drive?" Carstairs interrupted. Both Mr Walsh and Beryl stared at him in amazement. Mr Walsh jumped up and backed away until he bumped into the next table.

"How the bloody hell are you alive?" he shouted. Beryl reacted in a similar way.

"You're 'ead exploded!" she said, horrified. "I've still got bits of it in me hair and I'll never get the stains out of my favourite cardi."

"It's a long story..." began Carstairs.

"Aye," said Doctaroo. "An' you'll never guess what happened."

Mr Walsh sat down again. "I bet it was an android double designed to act as a decoy for any potential assassin's bullet," he said confidently. Doctaroo looked disappointed.

"Smart arse."

After long-winded explanations from both Mr Walsh and Carstairs and several cups of instant black coffee, Mr Walsh handed over the thumb drive. Carstairs handed it to the officer standing by the door and told him to get it analysed. He praised the bravery of Mr Walsh, who smiled modestly and Beryl, who didn't. Instead she demanded the attentions of a stylist and hairdresser. Assuring her that he would sort something out, he questioned them about the creatures in the photograph.

"Yeah," said Mr Walsh. "They call themselves the Kkrellem - with two Ks. They're from another dimension and they like to eat people."

"Oh god, yeah," said Beryl. "One of them wanted to eat me. Then someone on the phone said they could eat the receptionist instead!"

"Ugh," said Doctaroo. "I bet there wasn't much meat on her though."

"Oh, no. She was a stick insect! Not a pick on her."

"He said he was gonna barbecue her haunches," said Mr Walsh angrily.

"Gosh," said Maule-Ffinch. However did you escape?"

"Oh, Mr Walsh was dead brilliant. He pressed the fire alarm and they couldn't stand the noise."

"Armadillos have very sensitive hearing." said Mr Walsh. "Once the alarm started, they opened up the doorway thingy they used to get here and vanished back where they came from."

"Wait. Go back a bit. What doorway thingy?" asked Maule-Ffinch.

"It was a glowing, blue, hazy thing they opened in the mirror," said Beryl. "Like a portal in one of those Sci-Fi shows Brian watches."

"Yeah," said Mr Walsh. "Like a Stargate."

"Oh I love that show," Doctaroo interjected. "That Richard Dean Anderson is flippin' gorgeous!"

Carstairs ignored her. "You say it opened in the mirror?" he asked. Beryl nodded.

"Yeah. It was one of those ornate full length ones on a stand. Like in Downton, y'know?" A frown crossed her face fleetingly. "I'd been checking my make-up in it when it started glowing at the edges."

"That was after we found the camera though," said Mr Walsh.

Carstairs pointed to the photographs. "Yes, we know about the cameras. We had them installed last week under the pretence of a maintenance inspection. We had to replace the art on the walls with reproductions painted onto one-way mirrors."

Mr Walsh looked at Beryl, who looked at the floor, the walls, the ceiling... In fact, anywhere but back at Mr Walsh. He licked his lips.

"The paint was still wet. It would have fooled no one," he said and pretended that he suddenly had a very dry mouth and went off to get some more water.

Carstairs watched him walk away an expression of puzzled curiosity on his face.

"What did he mean by that?" he asked Beryl. She shrugged and responded with her best smile

"Never mind," said Carstairs as an officer handed him a file. He opened it and skimmed through its contents.

"Interesting," he murmured. "Here." He passed the file to Maule-Ffinch.

Maule-Ffinch opened it. "I say," he said in surprise. "That can't be right."

"Exactly," replied Carstairs. "Unfortunately, a single reference can't be used as evidence."

Beryl put up her hand. Doctaroo leant in and whispered, "You don't have to put your hand up pet. We're not at school."

Beryl put it down again. "But don't you want to know what I was going to say?" she asked.

Doctaroo shrugged. "Oh I'm not really bothered, hinnie. Unless you were going to suggest going out or to a party or something."

"Actually, I think I can help there," said Carstairs. He turned to Beryl. "I presume you were going to ask what is in this file."

She nodded.

"It makes mention of the real purpose of Noor's pipeline," Carstairs went on. "Unfortunately it doesn't go into detail, it's just a fleeting reference in an email. However, it does say that all the blueprints, both real and official are stored on an old-school floppy disk in Noor's home safe."

"Why the hell would he use a floppy disk?" asked Henry incredulously. "Who uses floppies these days?"

"I've had my fair share of floppies, I can tell you," snorted Doctaroo.

"Yes, thank you Doctaroo. I'm sure nobody is interested in your love life," sighed Carstairs.

"Nooo," said Doctaroo scathingly. "I mean my Trydis uses them. Five and a quarter inch floppy disks. With all the travellin' I do, it's more convenient than the cloud."

"But that's perfect!" exclaimed Maule-Ffinch. "If we could somehow get hold of Noor's disk, then we could use Doctaroo's equipment to read what's on it!"

"Aww, champion," said Doctaroo. "All we need to do now is to get hold of the floppy. Although things don't usually stay floppy once I've got me hands on…"

"Yes, thank you Doctaroo. We get the gist," interrupted Carstairs. "As for obtaining the disk, I believe we've got that covered." He held up a gold envelope.

"This arrived this afternoon. We had to open it of course; security you understand. But it's addressed to you."

Chapter Ten.

Dr Noor was having a party. Among the guests were a number of Hollywood actors including, Charlize Theron, Sir Ian McKellen and Sir Kenneth Branagh. There were various members of Parliament, television stars – a good number from Noor's favourite show, Holby City – and several so-called personalities that Brian recognised from daytime television. And Christopher Biggins.

Plus, of course, Doctaroo, Beryl, Mr Walsh, Maule-Ffinch, Henry and himself.

Once Doctaroo had seen the invitation and loudly proclaimed that she "loved a party", she had then ran around like the proverbial headless chicken while muttering that she had nothing to wear. Carstairs concern about how Noor had known about Doctaroo's involvement considering he was supposed to know nothing about her, was enthusiastically dismissed by the person in question and her demands for a "suitable outfit for a swanky party" kind of superseded any and all questions regarding that matter.

Eventually a luckless copper was despatched to the nearest Primark (the offer to buy her something from Selfridges having been pooh-poohed scornfully by Doctaroo who declared that she didn't want anything from "that poncey shop") to purchase a simple black dress for her and Beryl and a couple of nice suits for Brian, Henry and Mr Walsh.

Once Brian had returned from his coffee run with lattes for everyone, a car had been swiftly organised to take them to Noor's cliff-side home in Portsmouth. There, they were greeted warmly by the host and had large glasses of vintage champagne pressed into their hands with the invitation to look around and mingle. Doctaroo, spotting Eammon Holmes chatting to the bloke off The Chase, gave a whoop of delight and hurried over to accost them both.

Mr Walsh, feeling conspicuous decided to get some air and went out to the large patio which overlooked the Olympic sized pool and beautifully tended gardens.

He walked along a path that took him around the pool and down a narrow flight of stone steps which ran down the cliff to the pebble beach below. Here, pulled up the beach where they were tied to a heavy iron ring embedded in the cliff face, were a number of watercraft that Mr Walsh assumed belonged to Dr Noor.

He ran his hand appreciatively over the hull of a classic wooden speedboat, its highly polished deck glistening in the evening sunshine. He was startled out of his reverie by the sound of raised voices from the cliff side steps. He ducked behind the speedboat as two figures ran down the steps and crunched their way across the beach to where a medium sized hovercraft sat.

The first figure he immediately recognised as Dr Noor, but he wasn't sure who the second person was. Noor opened the door to the cabin and climbed in. With an ear-splitting roar, the hovercraft's engine sprang into life, the bag instantly inflating. Noor's companion ran around the outside casting off the mooring lines that tethered the hovercraft to the iron ring.

Mr Walsh looked up as the sound of more running feet and shouts were barely to be heard over the hovercraft's engines. He squinted and could just make out the silhouettes of his friends against the setting sun. Doctaroo's voice could be heard yelling at Noor to stop. As they reached the hovercraft, its rear mounted fans spun faster and the compact vessel moved off along the beach to the cold waters of the Channel.

"Oh bugger!" shouted Doctaroo in frustration.

Mr Walsh popped up from behind the speedboat. "Oi, you lot! Over here!" he yelled and pointed at the boat. "We can go after him in this!"

Brian and Henry ran over to him, Maule-Ffinch close behind. Together they managed to drag the boat on its launching trolley down to the water's edge. Doctaroo and Beryl jumped in, while the others pushed it out until it floated free of the trolley, then they too got in. Mr Walsh pulled the cord on the outboard and the big engine fired up.

"How fast do you reckon this thing goes?" asked Brian

"Not as fast as that hovercraft I reckon," said Henry, taking the wheel. "They have the advantage of not creating drag, plus it has twin fans creating more pounds of thrust."

"It doesn't really matter," said Maule-Ffinch. "He's probably headed for the Isle of Wight. He has a house there."

"Righto," said Henry. "Cowes it is then!" He spun the wheel and pushed the throttle forward. The boat lifted its nose and sped off after the hovercraft, Henry increasing its speed until the vintage craft got up on plane and zoomed out across the Solent.

They had been travelling for about three quarters of an hour and Doctaroo had been unusually quiet. She just sat and watched Henry, an odd look in her eyes.

Mr Walsh leaned over. "Everything okay, Doctaroo?"

She shook her head. "I've been thinkin'," she said to no one in particular.

Brian laughed. "Watch out, guys. That's a danger sign right there!"

Doctaroo smiled. "I don't mean like that, bonny lad."

"What's up Doctaroo?" asked Beryl.

"Oh it's probably nothing," she said. All the while not taking her eyes off Henry. "I'm probably just being silly, you know how I get sometimes, pet."

"Well, just as long as we get to Cowes in one piece, I wouldn't worry about it," said Henry. "We have to get that gnu back from Noor before he has a chance to use it."

Maule-Ffinch looked strangely at him, then at Doctaroo. She nodded sadly.

"How do you know about the gnu?" he asked.

Henry glanced sideways at him. "Er, you told me earlier."

Maule-Ffinch shook his head. "No, I didn't. The only person I told was Doctaroo. And that was before I'd even met you. Plus," he continued. "How do you know that Noor is headed for Cowes?"

Henry's shoulders slumped. "Dammit," he said in annoyance. "One little mistake."

He took a small black box with a single flashing LED on it from the inside pocket of his jacket and stuck it onto the steering wheel. Then he snapped off the throttle lever.

Mr Walsh and Maule-Ffinch made a move towards him, but suddenly Henry pulled a small, very compact, snub-nosed weapon from his trouser pocket. He grinned at Doctaroo.

"I feel like a fool, I really do," laughed Henry, all trace of his Australian accent having vanished. "I really think that I could have fooled you

116

all the way. But, y'know, I can't oversee everything." He smiled knowingly at Doctaroo, who just stared blankly back at him. She shook her head. Henry sighed.

"*Oversee* everything?" he repeated. Doctaroo shrugged.

"Nope. Haven't the foggiest," she said.

"Oh for goodness sake," he said in exasperation. "*OVERSEE* everything!"

"Sorry pet," said Doctaroo. "You're gonna have to explain it to us. I just can't figure out what you're on about."

"Oversee! *Oversee!* It's a play on words. Oversee."

Doctaroo still looked blankly at him. Henry waved the gun angrily at her.

"OVERSEE! I'm The Overseer! Do you understand? The bloody Overseer!"

Maule-Ffinch leaned in close to Doctaroo's ear. "I think he's called The Overseer, Doctaroo."

"The overseer Doctaroo? That's an odd name," she said, puzzled. I'm Doctaroo and I've heard of The Overseer. He's my arch enemy. You

117

can't be him though 'cos he's an old bloke with a bald head and bushy sideburns. He dresses funny too," she frowned and tried to make sense of the situation.

Unfortunately, the part of her brain that dealt with rational thought had gone on a package holiday to Lanzarote and left its booze sodden uncle in charge. Doctaroo dribbled slightly and went a little cross-eyed.

"Is the overseer Doctaroo the fella who taught The Overseer at school?" She gave a silly grin.

Henry was almost hopping up and down in frustration. "No, I'm The Overseer. Just. The. Overseer!"

"Ohhhh," said Doctaroo, the uncle must have called the holiday reps and got a message through because the penny finally dropped. "Well why didn't you just say that instead of all that messing about?"

Henry just stared at her, mouth agape. "I hate you," he said quietly. "I really hate you. You are *the* most annoying person I have ever met. *Ever*."

"Well, that's not very nice, is it?" she said, looking around at her friends. As one they all shook their heads.

"Right, fine," said Henry, putting on a life jacket. "It doesn't matter anyway. The steering is locked and the boat is on a direct heading for the Isle of Wight. If my calculations are correct, which they are, then you should literally have a smashing time when you get there."

Doctaroo burst out laughing. "Oh, I get that one!" she said. "Smashing, because we're going to smash onto the rocks!"

Henry tried to ignore her. "I'd stick around but there's a helicopter en-route to pick me up." He stopped suddenly and looked incredulously at Doctaroo.

"Seriously, you got the smashing joke but completely missed the overseer thing?"

Doctaroo shrugged again and gave him her sweetest smile in a "what can I say" kind of way.

Henry inflated the life jacket and climbed up onto the prow.

"Well, I won't say it's been a pleasure, because it hasn't. I hope you all die in agony, especially you, Doctaroo." He paused, then got a small communication device from his other trouser pocket.

"In fact, I've had an idea." He turned on the communicator and spoke in a harsh alien language into it.

"Right then Doctaroo," he said "I've arranged for some friends to collect you. The rest of you? Rest in pieces."

With that, he jumped overboard, just as a helicopter flew overhead. It hovered over Henry who was treading water and lowered a rope which Henry put around his chest. He waved at the man inside who winched it back into the chopper, its passenger gripping on tightly. Once he was aboard, the helicopter banked sharply and flew back to the mainland.

Doctaroo turned and was about to say something when suddenly, a patch of light opened in the darkening sky, its glowing whiteness obstructing their view of the stars. The patch grew larger and just as suddenly a beam of light shot down from the heavens and engulfed Doctaroo.

"Oh dear." she said quietly and then she vanished, the beam of light vanishing just as quickly as it came.

"Okay, said Mr Walsh. "Well, that just happened."

Maule-Ffinch dived into the driving seat and began wrestling with the controls.

"It's no good," he said, desperation creeping into his voice. "I can't shift it."

"It's that box thing he attached to the steering wheel," said Mr Walsh. "It's affecting the controls somehow. Can you try to remove it?"

Maule-Ffinch reached out to touch the box. There was a flash of blue sparks and he snatched back his hand with a yelp. He looked up at Mr Walsh.

"That'll be a firm *no*."

The boat continued to speed across the Solent towards the Isle of Wight. Closer and closer it drew until the cliffs and rocks came into view. Beryl moved up to the front and pointed at the rapidly approaching shoreline.

"Well, if you're gonna do somethin', now's the time to do it! We're gonna crash!" she screamed...

Chapter Eleven.

Doctaroo awoke from a dreamless sleep to find herself lying on a makeshift bunk in a rough stone building. She sat up and took stock of her surroundings. There was a wooden table and two chairs sited under a small multi-paned window. Next to the window was a heavy oak door on thick iron hinges and latched with a solid iron bolt. Beside the door was a couple of hooks that held a twelve bore shotgun and a leather satchel.

She got up and walked over to a heavy Walsh dresser that stood against the wall next to the gun. On top of the dresser was a large ceramic bowl with a matching jug of water beside it. Doctaroo poured some of the water into the bowl and splashed it on her face. She grabbed a rough towel from a hook on the dresser and dried her face and hands.

She walked over to the table to find a small plate with some coarse bread and a hunk of dried up cheese on it. Beside this was a ceramic bottle with the legend 'Wm Younger's Light Pale Ale' printed on the label.

Doctaroo pulled off a piece of bread and stuffed it greedily into her mouth, followed by a chunk of the cheese and then she washed it down with a swig of the beer.

"Aah," she sighed. "Champion."

The door opened and a handsome young man of around nineteen years of age walked in. He stopped and smiled broadly at Doctaroo.

"You're awake," he said, in a soft Northumbrian accent. "We were worried you would be unconscious for some time."

"Aye, pet. Could you tell me where I am? Doctaroo smiled at him.

124

"Aye, miss. You're at Killingworth. My friends brought you here last night, just after midnight," the young man said. "My father had them put you in here so you could sleep undisturbed."

"My thanks to you both," replied Doctaroo. "It's a pleasure to meet such a handsome young man. What's your name, pet?"

The young man blushed. "Robert, miss. "I'm apprentice to Mister Wood, the colliery viewer here."

"The viewer?" asked Doctaroo.

"Aye, miss. he's in charge of the entire mine. I'll be leaving his employ soon, However. I'm going to work with my father in Darlington."

He stopped suddenly, his body racked with coughing. He dabbed his lips with a handkerchief and gave Doctaroo an apologetic smile.

"Sorry about that, miss. I've not been right since an accident down the mine."

"Don't worry about that pet, I'm always having accidents. Tena Lady usually works for me though."

Robert gave her a blank look.

"Mind you," she went on. "You'd be better off with Tena Men, I suppose. There's a bigger surface area for…" she waved her hand vaguely around her lower torso, "…you know, down there." Her voice dropped to a whisper for the last two words.

Whether it was her tone of voice or just the way she indicated her nether regions, Robert must have understood her because he blushed a vivid red.

"Oh, no miss. It's nothing like that. There was an explosion you see, down the pit. The doctor reckons I have weak lungs and that all the dust in the mine has affected it. He thinks I might have a touch of consumption."

"Oh, I get that too," said Doctaroo completely misunderstanding. "Oh yeah, I often suffer from excessive consumption. Consumption of broon ale mostly, like!"

Robert laughed. "Well, I'm due down the pit with Mister Wood, but we usually go to the Three Tuns afterwards for a herring, a penny roll and a glass of beer. You'd be very welcome to join me."

126

Doctaroo gave him a seductive smile. "Are you asking me out, young Robert? I'm old enough to be your Gran… erm your Mam… um, your sister."

Robert blushed again. "I think you're teasing me miss."

Doctaroo punched him playfully on the arm. "Just a little bit."

Robert opened the door. "I have to go, miss. You're welcome to go outside, I'd steer clear of the pit, mind. It can get a little dangerous. And don't go near the machinery either, it's Mr Wood's baby. He wouldn't appreciate you touching it."

"Oh don't worry about that, pet. Me and machinery don't really get along."

Robert nodded and left. Doctaroo finished the beer and set the bottle down on the table.

"Right then," she said rubbing her hands together. "Time to have a shufti at where I've ended up."

She opened the door carefully and peered cautiously out. It was basically your bog-standard, nineteenth century coal mining village.

I'm not going to go into detail, if you really want to know, google it! Or better still, go to your local library and look it up. Who do you think I am anyway, your bloody history teacher? Anyway, Doctaroo goes out and has a look around the village.

I'll be coming back to this a little later, but first we're going to nip forward a couple of centuries and see how Brian, Beryl and the others managed to escape certain death by being dashed onto the rocks just off the Isle of Wight. For those of you who don't fancy that, you can always skip forward to a later chapter which is really exciting and has Ian Fleming and the Queen in it.

Chapter Twelve.

Brian dragged himself from the freezing waters of the Solent and staggered up the beach to where Beryl, Mr Walsh and Maule-Ffinch were sitting on the sea wall, wringing out their sodden clothing. He sat down next to Beryl and gazed out at the wreckage of the speedboat as it washed up on the shore.

Realising that there was no way they were going to be able to turn the boat away from the rocks, or slow it down, Mr Walsh had made the decision to jump overboard and swim for it. He had then grabbed the only life jacket on board and pulled it over Beryl's head. Then passing Brian and Maule-Ffinch a couple of the inflatable cushions from a locker at the back of the boat and taking one for himself, he made sure that Beryl's life jacket was fully inflated as were the cushions and made each one of them jump off the transom and into the murky waters of the Channel before following suit himself.

The speedboat had roared onwards toward the cliffs and with an enormous crash, it smashed itself to pieces on the jagged rocks at the bottom.

"Aww hey, that's just typical that is," moaned Beryl, holding up a small pocket mirror and surveying what the salt water had done to her hair. "This 'do cost me five pounds, eleven and six at Herbert's in Aigburth last week."

Brian shrugged. "So? A fiver is cheap for a haircut. *Really* cheap."

"Ah, that was back in 1965, mate," said Mr Walsh. You're talking around ninety quid in today's money."

"Ninety eight pounds, twenty two pence actually," said Maule-Ffinch absently. The others stared at him. He blushed.

"Pater is a bit of an amateur numismatist," he stammered by way of an explanation.

"Who's Peter when he's at home?" demanded Beryl.

"Not Peter, dumbo." Brian said scathingly. "He said Pater."

"Oh yeah?" said Beryl, bristling. "An' what does *that* mean then, smartarse?"

"He means his dad," said Mr Walsh stepping between them. "It's what posh people call their old man."

"I call my old man from the phone box at the bottom of Pilch Lane," laughed Beryl. "I've had to ever since me mam chucked him out."

"Was he diddling the gas meter again?" laughed Mr Walsh.

"That's not all he was diddlin'" Beryl replied. "Turns out he was carrying on with that Peggy Kelly from number fifty four too."

They both laughed long and hard at this, Brian offering a noncommittal shrug to Maule-Ffinch by way of saying "Nope, I've no idea what they're on about either."

Maule-Ffinch cleared his throat. "Right, well, yes indeed."

Brian and Beryl stopped laughing, although they tried forlornly not to catch each other's eye for fear of starting again. Maule-Ffinch gave a wan smile.

"I think that our next call to action would be to attempt to contact DCI Carstairs. Wouldn't you agree?" They nodded.

"Oh yeah, definitely." Brian agreed. But how? My phone's at the bottom of the Channel."

Maule-Finch pursed his lips. "Mine's ruined too."

"And mine," said Mr Walsh. "So what do you suggest?

"Well, I think we ought to take a leaf from Beryl's book and go and find a phone box."

Noor stood looking out of his penthouse window at the twinkling lights of the city below. He sipped expensive whisky from a crystal tumbler, allowing the golden aromatic liquid to slosh over his tongue and swirl around his mouth, appreciating its oaky, peaty smokiness.

"Hmm," he mused as he detected complex notes of vanilla and grape. "Finished in sherry casks if I'm not mistaken," he thought before swallowing slowly, letting the fiery elixir burning a path through his oesophagus to his stomach where it spread a familiar warmth throughout his body.

"Sheer nectar," he said reverently as he took another sip.

The door opened and Renifler walked into the room. He crossed the deep pile carpet and stood next to his employer.

"You're late," said Noor. "You should have been at Portsmouth to meet my hovercraft. As it was, I had to telephone for an Uber to take me home."

Renifler gave a half-shrug. "It was unavoidable, M'sieur. I was delayed rescuing

M'sieur McLachlan from the sea and taking him back to the London office."

"McLachlan? Has he resurfaced then?"

"Oui, M'sieur," replied Renifler. "He instructed me to tell you that he has dealt with Doctaroo and her colleagues."

Noor breathed a sigh of relief. "Oh fantastic. That's a relief."

He poured himself another glass of Scotch and offered one to Renifler. The Frenchman politely declined.

"Non, merci. I never drink alcohol before an assignment, I prefer to keep a clear head."

"Suit yourself," said Noor draining the glass. "Personally I intend to get completely smashed."

Renifler looked at him disdainfully. He was beginning to think that M'sieur le Overseer was correct in his estimation of Noor's character. Perhaps Noor really had outlived his usefulness after all. Renifler felt a warmth spreading throughout his body and quickly checking to make sure he hadn't soiled himself again, he allowed himself to enjoy the feeling knowing deep within his flint-like heart that he might soon have the pleasure of putting a bullet between Noor's eyes. Or perhaps, if he was feeling extra generous, he would suffocate him while he slept. Or better still, if time permitted, he would rig Noor's car to explode the next time he started its engine.

Happily contemplating Noor's impending execution, Renifler joined the object of his morbid bloodlust in gazing out at the London skyline.

"It seems so..." he began.

"Peaceful?" asked Noor. Renifler shook his head.

"Non," he said softly. "Unsuspecting. They have no idea what lies ahead for them."

"Does that thought please you?" Noor asked, slightly disturbed by the glint in the Frenchman's eye. Or was it a reflection off his steel nose? Either way it was quite chilling.

Renifler smiled humourlessly. "You have no idea."

Noor instinctively moved ever so slightly away from him and he glanced around for something he could use as a weapon if needed. His gaze alighted on a golden statuette of an African wildebeest he had recently bought at Sotheby's on the instructions of his employer.

He had no idea why The Overseer wanted it and when he had asked, his employer had refused to furnish him with a suitable explanation. All he had said was that it was a vitally important part of their current endeavour. His expression indicated that he would brook no further discussion, so Noor had obediently attended the auction and had successfully bid on the object d'art.

Personally, Noor thought that it was one of the ugliest things he had ever seen and he had unceremoniously dumped the statuette on the sideboard behind a model of the Eiffel Tower and a Zuni doll he'd been given by an ex-girlfriend.

He wondered how much the statuette weighed. It was apparently solid gold, so he imagined it would do considerable damage if smashed into someone's cranium.

If Renifler got any weirder, he thought, then perhaps he'd find out just how much damage that was.

Chapter Thirteen.

Doctaroo had happily spent the morning wandering around Killingworth like a tourist on the first day of their holiday to Spain, before the novelty of the "old town" wore off and they spent the rest of their vacation in the nearest English bar and looking for somewhere that did a decent portion of fish and chips.

She saw Robert approaching from the direction of the pit head and waving to him, she ran to meet him outside the small building that served as the mine's local watering hole.

"Howay, pet," she called, stopping breathlessly in front of him. "It's your round!"

Robert grinned and held open the door for her. Once inside, Doctaroo grabbed a stool and sat beside an old barrel that served as a table. Robert returned from the bar with two tankards of ale and a plate of boiled herring. He plonked them down on the table in front of her and then briefly went back to the bar, before coming back with two coarse bread rolls. He gave one to Doctaroo and sat down opposite her.

"Would you like some mustard, Miss?" He asked, holding out a small pot of some muddy yellow substance. Doctaroo shook her head.

"No thanks pet," she said, poking at the boiled fish with a knife. "I don't eat anything I can't identify properly."

Robert blobbed a spoonful of the mustard onto his plate. "Howay man, I've been looking forward to this."

He picked up a piece of fish, dipped it into the mustard and then stuffed it greedily into his mouth. He chewed vigorously for a moment, before breaking off a piece of bread roll and cramming it into his mouth to join the herring. He took a swig of ale to wash it down and then sighed happily.

"Eee, I love a man who enjoys his food!" exclaimed Doctaroo. Robert put a hand to his mouth and belched quietly.

"Excuse me," he said bashfully. "I've not eaten since yesterday morning."

Doctaroo looked concerned. "Why ever not?"

"Oh it's nothing to worry about, Miss," he explained. "I sometimes forget to eat if I'm busy." He glanced around suspiciously. "I'm not really supposed to say, but I've been working on summat special with Mr Wood."

Doctaroo leaned forward eagerly. "Ooh, what is it you're working on?" she whispered. "Is it top secret an' something you can't discuss on pain of death, or at the very least suffering a particularly painful Chinese Burn?"

Before Robert could answer, a booming voice could be heard from the doorway.

"Ah, there you are, young Stephenson! I thought I might find you here, whetting your whistle with a toby of brown ale."

Doctaroo turned to see who was speaking and gave a tiny gasp. The man was of average height and build with a bald head and thick, mutton chop sideburns that lent his face an air of professorial intelligence. He had pale blue eyes that were sad and yet somehow fierce at the same time. He had a long aquiline nose and a mouth that was kind and cruel in equal measures. He wore an expensive looking frock coat with straight trousers, a short waistcoat and a shirt with a high stiff collar. On his feet, he wore black patent leather boots.

Overall, he had a look sort of like a cross between Graeme Garden and Stalin, if Stalin was an early nineteenth century English land owner.

Robert jumped to his feet.

"Mr Wood, sir. May I introduce my companion...?" His voice tailed off as he realised that he had no idea of his companion's name. He needn't have worried however, as both parties looked at each other in mutual recognition.

Wood gave an elaborate bow and smiled warmly at Doctaroo.

"Why, Doctaroo. How delightful to see you again," he said, his voice like honey. Doctaroo just stared at him sadly.

"See?" she said to no one in particular. "I said he had a bald head and bushy sideburns."

Brian slurped noisily at the super large, triple whipped, full fat chocolate milkshake Maule-Ffinch had bought him to stop his extremely vocal complaints at not being able to sample any of the food at Noor's party the night before. In fact, he had used the credit card he had been given to cover any expenses incurred during his current assignment to buy them all breakfast at a small cafe on the sea front at Cowes.

Mr Walsh was mopping up the remains of his bacon and eggs with a piece of wholemeal toast, while Beryl was finishing off a sausage bap and washing it down with the steaming contents of a mug of tea.

Maule-Ffinch was sipping from a mug of hot brown liquid, not entirely like coffee and toying with something that was pretending to be scrambled eggs on toast, but that had a texture and colour more akin to wallpaper paste which, he suspected, would probably be a tad more palatable.

He had used the pay phone in the cafe to contact Carstairs who had immediately dispatched a helicopter to collect them and bring them back to Scotland Yard where they could plan their next move. The only thing they could do now was to wait until their transport arrived. Maule-Ffinch sipped at his not-quite-coffee and grimaced. What he wouldn't give, he thought, for a nice full-bodied Colombian. Or failing that, a cup of coffee.

He groaned inwardly. He'd definitely been spending too much time around Doctaroo.

The sound of an approaching helicopter interrupted his brooding and he silently gave thanks to the patron saint of civil servants for the welcome distraction it brought from such disturbing thoughts. He looked out of the large picture window at the chunky black Eurocopter EC155 that hovered overhead. As the tide was out, its pilot landed the chopper on the sand and waited for Maule-Ffinch and the others to run out to it.

Breathlessly they climbed aboard and once they were safely buckled in, the helicopter took off and flew back to the mainland.

Less than forty minutes later, they were safely back at Scotland Yard where Carstairs listened incredulously to their tale.

"So," Carstairs said after they had finished regaling him with their latest exploits. "What you're telling me is that McLachlan is really this Overseer chap who's in league with Dr Noor and that Doctaroo vanished from the deck of an out of control speedboat in a flash of light. Is that correct?"

Mr Walsh nodded vigorously. "Spot on, sunshine."

"And," continued Carstairs, "you have absolutely no idea as to where she has vanished?"

"God, you're dead quick aren't yer?" said Beryl, rolling her eyes. "I can see how you got to be so high up in the bizzies."

Carstairs ignored her sarcasm. "Did you manage to get the disc?"

Maule-Ffinch removed it from his suit jacket pocket. "Here you are Inspector. Although without Doctaroo, I don't see how we're going to be able to access the data that's stored on it."

"Is her Trydis still parked on the roof?" Brian asked.

"As far as I know, yes. But the door is locked and we've been unable to get into it." Carstairs replied.

Beryl's mouth fell open in shocked astonishment. "Why doesn't that surprise me eh? That's just typical of you lot. She's agreed to help you out and the first thing you do is try to break into her ship. Cheeky fuc..."

"Don't worry about that, Inspector," interrupted Brian, just in time to prevent an R rating. "I have a spare key. If you let me have the disc, I can try and access it via the on-board computer."

"Ha, you'll be lucky," laughed Mr Walsh. "That thing's about as powerful as a Sinclair ZX81."

"Nevertheless," said Carstairs, "I need to extract the data from the disc. So I suggest you accompany our tech specialist back to the Trydis and get it for me."

"Who's your tech guy?" asked Brian.

Carstairs took out his remote control and ran his fingers over the screen. A few seconds later the office door opened and ME2 walked in carrying a silver flight case.

"ME2 will assist you in retrieving the data," said Carstairs. "He has full specifications of pretty much every computer ever made programmed into his cerebellum."

"Computers made on Earth," corrected Mr Walsh.

"*Ever* made," insisted Carstairs. "Now, if you'll be on your way please," he said to ME2 and the others. "I have some arrangements to make concerning the opening ceremony of Noor's pipeline."

"Where is it to be held?" asked Maule-Ffinch.

"Blackfriars tube station. Or rather, what used to be Blackfriars tube station. Now it's the centre of operations for the pipeline." Carstairs sat back in his chair with a weary sigh. He pitched the bridge of his nose with the thumb and forefinger of his left hand.

"I'm responsible for the security of the VIP who's going to make the dedication and officially start the turbines."

"Who's that gonna be then?" demanded Beryl. Carstairs tapped the side of his nose.

"Blimey!" exclaimed Mr Walsh. "Barry Manilow's doing it?"

Carstairs did an actual double take. "What? No," he shot Mr Walsh a look that clearly indicated that he thought that the librarian was a few bricks short of a Lego set. "Of course it's not Barry Manilow. What the hell made you think it was him?"

"You tapped your nose, so I figured it was someone with a big nose. Obviously." Mr Walsh said defensively.

"Ooh, is it Ringo Starr?" asked Beryl excitedly. "I love him. Did you know he once asked our Maureen out? He said he wanted to take her up the Cavern, so she told him he had to buy her dinner first!" She burst into laughter.

"Didn't Maureen used to play the mouth organ?" asked Mr Walsh, supplying the feed line for a corny joke.

"No, that was our Monica," said Beryl, never one to waste a punchline.

"Look!" said Carstairs, massaging his temples as he could feel the beginnings of a migraine coming on. "It's not bloody Ringo Starr, it's not bloody Barry Manilow and it's not bloody anyone else with a big nose! I tapped *my* nose to indicate that it's none of your bloody business!"

"Well, if that's how yer gonna be, you can stick it right up *your* nose!" Beryl said haughtily. "Come on Brian, lad. We'll go back to the ship and let his majesty here plan his posh soirée."

She grabbed Brian's arm and dragged him from the room. Getting the nod from Carstairs, ME2 followed.

"Well, I don't know about you, Nigel mate. But I could do with a cup of proper coffee. That instant stuff at that café tasted like mud." He got up from the sofa and headed out the door.

"Coming?"

Maule-Ffinch glanced over at Carstairs who was busy swallowing several small white pills.

"Are you buying?" he asked.

Mr Walsh sighed. "Yeah, okay then. But none of your fancy flat white's or cinnamon Americanos."

"Fine by me," said Maule Ffinch. "All I want is a nice strong espresso or three to take the edge off."

Mr Walsh, who had spent some time in the company of what he'd come to realise was really just a small, sex-mad, slightly alcoholic whirling dervish, found that he could empathise fully with the tired depressed and dejected civil servant in front of him.

"It'll take more than an espresso to do that Nigel," he said cheerily, putting an arm across his shoulders and leading him from the room, "did I ever tell you about the time me, Doctaroo and Beryl were trapped behind a waterfall on the planet Quornquellous with a tribe of cannibalistic pygmies? We'd helped out a couple of missionaries from the Church of Latter Day Sternutamentums, who had crash landed several days earlier and the pygmies were set to roast them with seasonal vegetables and a piquant barbecue sauce…" His voice tailed off as they vanished down the corridor.

Carstairs picked up the telephone and dialled an outside number. He waited for a few seconds, drumming his fingers on the desk. Someone picked up the receiver at the other end.

"Yes? They said haughtily.

"It's me," said Carstairs. "Is everything arranged?"

"Of course," said the voice. "Everything is prepared. We await only the go ahead from your end."

Carstairs hung up. He needed a drink.

Chapter Fourteen.

Nicholas Wood was born in County Durham in 1795. He was a prominent steam locomotive and colliery engineer who helped George Stephenson in many of his engineering achievements including Stephenson's 'Geordie' lamp which predated Sir Humphrey Davy's safety lamp by only a month, something Davy was convinced could not have been a coincidence.

Such was Stephenson's respect for Wood that he sent his son Robert to become his apprentice in 1819.

However, the man who currently went by the name Nicholas Wood, colliery manager at Killingworth, was not the eminent historical engineer. He was, if you hadn't already guessed, an earlier aspect of Doctaroo's arch nemesis, The Overseer (don't worry, all will become clear later on - I told you it would be a doozy).

Doctaroo toyed with her boiled fish. The Overseer leaned forward and picked a piece off her plate and took a bite.

"You don't mind, do you?" he asked, chewing with his mouth open. "I skipped breakfast you see. Had to arrange your collection from 2020 at rather short notice. That's the trouble with future versions of yourself, everything has to be done immediately."

"Knock yourself out pet," said Doctaroo pushing the plate towards him. "Just do us a favour and close your mouth while you chew, eh. Nobody needs to see that."

She looked over at Robert who was still happily eating his lunch, then back at The Overseer.

"Should you be talkin' about the future an' stuff with him here?" she asked indicating the young man.

"Oh don't worry about him," said The Overseer. "Robert is very ahead of his time, quite the young prodigy really. He's destined for great things."

"Don't tell me," Doctaroo sneered. "You're here to put a stop to that."

"Oh, good heavens no!" exclaimed The Overseer. "I'm here to actively encourage it! You see, even though he doesn't yet know it, Robert here is going to help me with my most incredibly audacious scheme to date. A plan two hundred years in the making and which crosses not only the boundaries of time and space, but furthermore, across two different dimensions!"

Doctaroo yawned.

"Aye whatever, pet. You might wanna keep your voice doon though, people are starting to give you some reet funny looks."

The Overseer stood up and put a hand on Robert's shoulder. "Come along, Robert," he said almost completely failing to show no emotion. "I think it's time to show Doctaroo what we're doing here."

Robert jumped up. "Of course Mr Wood, if you reckon she's ready for it."

The Overseer smiled benignly at his protégée. "Oh, I think she's ready, my boy." He indicated to Doctaroo that she should go first. Reluctantly, she got up and headed for the door.

"You're not taking me to your kinky sex dungeon are you?" she asked over her shoulder. "One filled with whips an' chains an' lubrication products?"

"Certainly not!" exclaimed The Overseer.

"Oh well," Doctaroo said sadly. "Never mind. A girl can dream..."

Robert led them to the pit head where he showed them into the small manager's hut. Inside was a heavy walnut desk and leather captain's chair, a couple of plain chairs and a chest that sat under the window next to the door. The Overseer sat down

154

behind the desk and opened a small wooden box that sat to the side of the large blotter and inkwell that sat on top of the desk's leather lining and took out a fat cigar. He offered one to Doctaroo who shook her head.

"Suit yourself," he said lighting it. He took a puff and blew out a thick, grey smoke ring. "Hoyo de Monterrey Double Corona. Castro gifted me several boxes in the late nineteen sixties."

"Really? How interestin'," she lied. "So is this what you wanted to show me? A big fat smelly cigar? Mind you though, it's a rather apt description when you think about it. Considerin' who's smokin' it."

The Overseer just smiled and nodded to Robert who pulled a lever set into one of the walls. With a jolt, the room began to judder slightly and Doctaroo noticed that the view out the window started to slowly move upwards before giving way to what she realised was a stone lift shaft. After several minutes, the room stopped moving and she could see a dimly lit corridor through the window. Robert unlatched the door and held it open. The

Overseer jumped to his feet and ushered Doctaroo out.

The corridor turned out to be a tunnel, carved out of the rock by machinery well in advance of the century they currently occupied. Its sides were polished smooth like glass and there were fluorescent strip lights at regular intervals along its length.

The Overseer led the way and they walked through the tunnel until they reached a heavy metal door at the end. Robert spun the large wheel set about halfway up and the door swung open. Behind the door was a room the size of a small restaurant, its walls lined with pipes and valves all linked to complex and, for the time, incredibly advanced machinery. Working at the machinery were several creatures: half man, half armadillo, who wore what appeared to be gladiator costumes.

Doctaroo recognised them as the same creatures that had taken her from the speedboat earlier. The Overseer hurried forwards, pointing at the creatures.

"Have you met the Kkrellem?" he asked rhetorically. "Lovely chaps when

you get to know them. A bit fierce looking with a penchant for eating people, but smashing fellas really."

He went around the room introducing each one to her.

"This is Kkrask, he's the leader I suppose," he said pointing to the biggest creature. "Over there is his brother Kkrank. That's Kkrogh, he's another brother. And him over there, his name is Kkrell. He's also their brother." He turned to Kkrask. "Are you all related?"

Kkrask smiled, showing several rows of needle-like teeth. "We are born four to a brood. Kkrank, Kkrogh, Kkrell and I are of the same brood. Kkrukh and Kkroth are of a different brood as evidenced by the colour of their crests."

"Well, there you go," said The Overseer. "That explains it."

"Ooh, are you all so muscly?" asked Doctaroo saucily.

"I've been working out," said Kkrask.

The Overseer shook his head in amazement. "Really?" he asked her incredulously. "Even anthropomorphic armadillos? Seriously?"

"Only the really muscly ones," said Doctaroo with a giggle. She gave Kkrask a crafty wink.

The Overseer hit the side of his head with his palm, as if trying to knock the image of the dumpy bespectacled Doctaroo with the scaly, hairy armadillo-like Kkrask.

"Well, that's a picture I'll be stuck with for the rest of my lives," he said queasily, walking to the far end of the room. He beckoned Doctaroo and Robert over and pointed to a large ornate full-length mirror on the wall.

"This is what we've been working on," he said with a smile. "This is what brought you here."

Doctaroo scratched her nose and gave him a scornful look. "Are you havin' an episode love?" she asked gently. "Would you like me to get someone for you?"

"What? No! Look, do you really have to be so patronising?" The Overseer looked hurt

"But pet," said Doctaroo, as kindly as she could. "It's just a big mirror. It's a lovely one, mind," she added quickly. "But the idea's been around for centuries."

"It's not just a mirror, for heaven's sake!" shouted The Overseer. "It's an inter-dimensional, multi-temporal, bi-directional corridor!"

"Oh well I knew that!" said Doctaroo, gesturing at the mirror. "I said to myself, 'Doctaroo,' I said. 'That's a bi-dri dresional multi-whatsit if ever I saw one'." she blustered. "I was just checkin' that *you* knew what it was."

The Overseer stared at her for a moment, then he turned around and walked over to one of the other Kkrellem who was affixing a heavy golden statuette onto a polished wooden plinth.

"Have you finished, Kkrukh?" he asked. The Kkrellem glanced up from his work.

"I have encased the device within the golden shell of the beast icon," he growled. "Although I still do not understand why I need to do this. It would be more expedient to simply send the mechanism through the gateway to the future."

159

"I've already explained that to you," sighed The Overseer. "It's a plot device. If we don't have the statue, then the title of the book makes no sense."

"But why must we leave it in this time period?" Kkrukh asked.

"Again," said The Overseer, as though he was addressing a small child. "It's to advance the story. I'm sending it to Napoleon Bonaparte so that in two hundred years it'll be worth a small fortune at auction. I've got to earn a living somehow."

He looked back at Doctaroo for support, but she gave him a look that said, 'you're on your own, mate', and then pretended to be distracted by a series of steam valves and dials on the wall beside her.

Kkrank approached Kkrask. "I believe that one would like to mate with you," he growled, indicating Doctaroo.

"Indeed," replied Kkrask. "However I feel such a liaison would prove to be fruitless. While her physiognomy is not entirely repulsive, I doubt her physiology would be able to withstand our mating rituals."

Kkrank snorted. "Your response begs the question as to why you would even consider mating with food!"

Kkrask sighed. "Brother, the day will come when you will understand that not all humans are food."

"Humans are cows, cows are food. You are getting soft, brother," hissed Kkrank. "First you converse with the humans, now you consider the possibility of mating with them?"

"It was you who broached the subject," began Kkrask. Kkrank snorted his disapproval and returned to his work. Kkrask watched Doctaroo carefully, strange conflicting thoughts whirling through his mind. The humans of this world, he thought, were very different from the ones of his own. They were more intelligent, had sophisticated communication skills. The one called Robert even had surprisingly advanced knowledge of their steam technology.

Kkrask mused on this thought for a moment. Kkrank and his other brothers had little time for humans, seeing them as merely food or, if fortune favoured them, as slaves. But Kkrask was different. The humans in Noor's office had shown compassion and sympathy for their fellows, something that the Kkrellem believed to be impossible. However, Kkrask had seen this with his own eyes and they had been opened to the possibility that the humans of Earth were not as his people saw them.

He wanted to know more.

Chapter Fifteen.

Renifler stood next to a large full length
mirror that was hung on one of the walls of the
advanced laboratory that occupied what used to be
the ticket office of Blackfriars underground station.
He checked his watch. His employer was late.

The surface of the mirror rippled and began
to glow. As the glow increased in intensity, the
rippled surface gave way to a whirling, swirling
vortex.in the far distance, Renifler saw a tiny shape
forming. It moved closer, gathering speed as it flew
towards him. Eventually, as it came nearer, Renifler

saw that it was one of the strange alien beings that operated the machinery in the tunnels below.

Kkrogh stepped from the gateway and snarled at Renifler. "Where is the cow called Noor?" it demanded.

"He's busy," replied Renifler. "I've been assigned to assist you."

Kkrogh looked him up and down. "Are you acquainted with our technology?"

"Technology?" sneered Renifler. "I'd hardly call nineteenth century steam engines technology!"

"A typical response that I expect from a cow. You lack the intelligence to fully understand Kkrellem technology."

Renifler squared up to him. "M'sieur, you and I do not know each other well enough to trade insults." He smiled coldly. "So on this occasion I will overlook your ignorance. However, if you refer to me as a cow again then I will probably shoot you."

Kkrogh stared at him for a moment, then burst into laughter. "Ha-ha, you have courage little human. I think I like you!"

"Believe me, M'sieur. The feeling is not mutual."

Renifler barged past the giant creature and walked back the way he had come. Kkrogh snorted in amusement and followed after him.

The secondary control centre of the pipeline was a large, white, hexagonal room with a vaulted ceiling – a hangover from its tube station origins. In the middle, arranged around its perimeter, were six mushroom shaped podiums made of some shiny silver metallic alloy. Atop these podia were mounted complex control units, bedecked with dials and switches and lights.

On the wall behind each mushroom was an illuminated panel filled with similar dials and switches. At one point the wall's surface was broken by an illuminated alcove housing a glass cylinder that stood from floor to ceiling.

At every console stood a Kkrellem, each one absorbed in whatever task it was they were undertaking. In the middle of the podiums stood a larger mushroom – the main console.

As they entered the room, Renifler's mobile rang. "Oui?" he said, answering it. It was Noor.

"Renifler, my dear fellow. How are we doing?"

"As well as can be expected. Le Directeur has sent a Kkrellem supervisor to spy on me, but that is irrelevant. We are on course for le lancement demain."

"Excellent Mr Renifler. You have excelled yourself as usual." Noor sounded delighted. "I am on my way to a small get together at number ten, the PM wants me to explain our system to the French and the Germans. Have you informed The Overseer of your progress?"

Renifler laughed. "Which Overseer, M'sieur?"

"Ah yes," said Noor slowly. "Which one indeed. I had quite forgotten about Mr McLachlan. Is he still at Canary Wharf?

Renifler sat down at one of the six consoles around the main central console where Kkrogh was busy studying the various computer read outs fed to his station by the other six units. His fingers played a digital symphony across a keyboard set into the console unit and a video feed from Noor's office was displayed. On the screen Henry could be seen watching a rugby match on Noor's eighty-five inch Sony television set, bottle of lager in one hand and bowl of nachos in the other. At one point, Henry lifted the bowl to his lips and grabbed a mouthful of chips, then took a swig of beer.

"Oui. He is, as you say, making himself at home." Renifler switched off the video feed. "Should I telephone him?"

There was a long pause then Noor spoke, a note of caution in his voice.

"No, I don't think so. Contact the other one via the temporal communicator. He seems to be the more stable version. Did you bring the statue from my penthouse?"

"Oui, bien sûr. It has been installed as per your instructions." Renifler looked across to the alcove containing the glass cylinder.

Inside, on an onyx plinth was the statuette of the golden gnu. A myriad of fibre optic cables wound and twisted around its gilded surface, each connected to its base via a platinum interface.

Noor was pleased. Barely able to keep the excitement from his voice, he almost giggled with joy.

"Oh this is going to so be worth it! Is the temporal connection stable?"

Renifler got up and crossed over to Kkrogh's station. He nudged the Kkrellem to one side and peered at the readout on the VDU.

"It appears to be. I will confirm it with The Overseer when I contact him later, but from what I can determine from the instruments, the connection to the Kkrellem vessel seems to be at full strength.

"Excellent," said Noor happily. "Just think, Renifler. We're actually going to be drawing energy directly from two hundred years ago. Never mind the geothermal energy they *think* we're using to heat the pipeline, *this* is the future! Right here and now and, of course, back then too! If this doesn't net me the Nobel Prize, then I don't know what will. I'll

168

contact you again tomorrow once I'm en route to the launching ceremony for the pipeline. Any problems or questions are to be directed to The Overseer, not McLachlan. I'll be incommunicado until then."

"Très bien, docteur Noor. Au revoir." Renifler ended the call and slipped the phone into his inside jacket pocket. He made to leave the control room but Kkrogh stepped in front of him and blocked his exit.

"That was the Noor cow..." He caught himself and started again. "The Noor person?" He seemed to have difficulty getting the right words out, which secretly delighted the stoic Renifler.

"If you mean *Doctor* Noor, then yes it was," he said with just a soupçon of pomposity.

"Is he coming here?" Kkrogh asked.

"Tomorrow," replied Renifler. "Why?"

The Kkrellem shifted his weight from one foot to the other. He seemed almost nervous, as though he was afraid of something. Renifler found this most perplexing. From the moment he had arrived, Kkrogh's manner was that of arrogance and tremendous power, yet here he was almost trembling with apprehension.

"I have information to impart to him." Kkrogh said.

"Is it important?" asked Renifler.

Kkrogh nodded. "Yes."

"That is unfortunate," said Renifler with a sneer. These Kkrellem were pathetic and fully deserved the fate The Overseer had in store for them. Noor also. Renifler felt a frisson of excitement run down his spine as he imagined how Noor would meet his end. He would relish the deaths of Kkrogh and his fellow Kkrellem, hopefully at his own hand, but he would savour every second of Noor's.

Kkrogh's attention was diverted by the flashing of a small red light on his console. He tapped the dial and barked a command at one of the other Kkrellem.

"Maintain observation of the pressure level in zone three! It must not go above forty nine psi." He stepped back to the main console. "There is a fluctuation in the coolant in observation booth nine.

Temperature must be kept below sixteen degrees centigrade."

There was a bleep from the communication panel.

Renifler thumbed a switch. "Oui, rapport s'il vous plaît."

There was a garbled babble from the speaker. Renifler glanced up at Kkrogh.

"What are they saying?"

Kkrogh pushed him away from the panel and spoke into the mic.

"What is happening?" The voice spoke again, a guttural mixture of clicks, snarls and whistles. Kkrogh replied in the same language.

Renifler straightened his tie and glared at the Kkrellem.

"You are not of this Earth, so I will allow you a certain leeway regarding your lack of manners. But I am growing weary of your tone when you address me and I would also sincerely advise you never to touch me like that ever again, M'sieur."

Kkrogh barely acknowledged him, dismissing his warning with a terse,

"Silence, cow!"

Renifler sighed quietly and closed his eyes. He counted to ten in his head, then drew his Glock and put six bullets into the Kkrellem's head. He pushed Kkrogh's lifeless body off the console and it fell to the floor with a thud. Renifler spoke into the mic.

"Votre attention s'il vous plaît," he cleared his throat. "M'sieur l'Overseer, I have some unfortunate news."

There was a short pause and then The Overseer's voice replaced that of the Kkrellem who had spoken to Kkrogh.

"What have you done now, Renifler?"

"It was unavoidable, M'sieur. Kkrogh's head got in the way of some bullets I accidentally fired from my gun," Renifler explained matter-of-factly. "I am extremely sorry."

"Oh very well," replied The Overseer. "But I'm going to let *you* explain it to his brothers."

"As you wish, M'sieur." Renifler checked that he had a spare clip. The Overseer's tone brightened.

"I must say, this communicator works wonderfully well, doesn't it?" he said cheerfully. "You sound as though you're just in the next room, rather than two hundred years in the future."

"Non, M'sieur," corrected Renifler. "I fear you are mistaken. It is *you* who is two hundred years in the *past*."

There was silence from the communicator. Then,

"I'm going to hang up now, Renifler. I want you to go away and think about what you've just said."

There was a click and the communicator switched off. Renifler gazed down at the body of the late Kkrellem, Kkrogh. He decided that instead of requesting a replacement, he would promote one of the lower grade technicians to acting supervisor. In the meantime, he thought placing a hand onto his stomach, he would just pop down to the commissary for a sandwich and a coffee. For a reason he had yet to fathom out, killing always gave him an appetite. He felt that oh so familiar warmth spread throughout his body.

Luckily, this time he was within reach of a lavatory.

Doctaroo was rather unhappy. Partly it was due to the presence of her arch nemesis, The Overseer. Partly it was due to being stuck in the nineteenth century. But mostly it was due to being locked in a tiny six foot square cell and tied to an uncomfortable wooden chair, made all the more uncomfortable by the almost unbearable itch she had developed in her left buttock. She wriggled around, trying in vain to scratch it somehow on the chair's rough seat.

There was the sound of a key rattling in the lock and the door swung open to reveal a nervous, and not a little frightened, Robert. The young engineer ran forwards, took out a pocket knife and began sawing at the ropes.

"Please forgive me, Miss, he whispered. "But I cannot, nay, *will not* stand by and allow any harm to come to thee. Especially not if I've had a hand in deceiving you."

174

The rope snapped and Doctaroo rubbed her wrists where it had chafed the skin. "Never mind, pet," she said kindly. "Divvent worry yourself about it."

Robert hung his head and wrung his hands. "Nevertheless, Miss. I feel that I've wronged you and I dearly wish to make amends. I really cannot understand what came over Mr Wood. He was always a kind, fair man without a bad word for anyone."

Doctaroo took Robert's hands in hers. "It's not your fault, pet," she said. "That man isn't Mr Wood. He's an imposter from the future who's been plotting some nefarious plans, probably to take over the world, or at the very least, the south-west of England."

"But, whatever happened to the real Mr Wood? Robert asked.

Doctaroo looked even more uncomfortable than when she was tied to the chair.

"Oh, don't you worry yourself about it," she said hoping her voice sounded a lot more cheerful that she felt. "I'm certain he'll show up at some point, she said, crossing her fingers behind her back.

Robert held a hand up, suddenly. "Shh, I can hear footsteps." He went over and put his ear to the door. "I hear voices too. I fear it is Mr Wood and one of those creatures."

He looked around the room desperately, but there was nowhere to hide. "Quick," he said pointing at the chair. "Sit back down and pretend to be tied up."

She sat down, her hands behind her back. Robert pressed himself as flat as he could against the wall at the side of the door. It opened and The Overseer and Kkrask entered the room. The Overseer stopped in front of Doctaroo, who stuck out her tongue at him.

Robert, who had been concealed from view by the open door, cautiously came out of hiding and approached The Overseer out of breath, pretending to have just ran in.

"Mr Wood, sir," he panted, quite convincingly too thought Doctaroo. "There's a problem at the pit head."

"What kind of problem?" asked The Overseer.

Robert shrugged. "I divvent know sir," he said. "They just said to come and get you."

"Can't Mr Samuels deal with it? I'm rather busy."

"No, sir," insisted Robert. "He's the one who's asking for you."

"Oh for goodness sake!" sighed The Overseer impatiently. Doctaroo grinned up at him.

"Aww, going so soon, pet?" she asked cheekily. "And we didn't even have time for a chat."

The Overseer suddenly bent down to her so that their noses were almost touching.

"Oh there'll be plenty of time for chatting when I get back!" he sneered. "And when I do..." He broke off and ran the index finger of his right hand across his neck in a slicing gesture.

"What? You're gonna cut your own throat? That's a bit daft isn't it?" asked Doctaroo.

"No, of course not," began The Overseer. "I'm miming... I'm going to..." He threw his hands up and let out a cry of frustration. "Gaaah! You are *so* annoying!

He turned and stormed out of the room.

Kkrask stepped up to Doctaroo. "Why do you anger him so?"

Doctaroo laughed. "Because it's a laugh, isn't it."

Kkrask tilted his head to one side and said, "I do not understand."

Doctaroo sighed and regarded the Kkrellem with a smile. "It's because it's funny. You know, it makes me giggle. It beats sitting around moping anyway."

Kkrask nodded. "I see," he said slowly. "It is for your amusement?"

Doctaroo grinned. "Aye, pet. That's right. It's all for fun."

"But do you not consider the danger you may face by doing such a thing? He is a dangerous human cow, as I have witnessed for myself," cautioned Kkrask.

"Howay, man," laughed Doctaroo. "He's about as dangerous as a blimmin' chinchilla."

178

"Perhaps," said Kkrask slowly. "But even a chinchilla can be lethal when armed with a blaster."

"Really?" said a surprised Doctaroo. "I didn't know they made blasters for chinchillas. They must be really wee guns mind, 'cos they've only got little hands."

She mimed holding a gun with really small hands. "Pew, pew, pew..." She gave Kkrask a scornful look. "Nah that would never happen. I mean, where would they keep their ammunition?"

"You are a curious human, cow," Kkrask murmured.

"...they've got no pockets for a start..." She stopped and looked both hurt and just a little angry. "What do you mean 'cow'?"

Kkrask ignored her. "I am most intrigued by your species," he said. "Unlike the humans of my world, you actually seem to be almost intelligent. More so, you appear to be able to show compassion, although the consensus is that you are merely mimicking the behaviour of other more superior species."

"Well now you're just being rude!" bristled Doctaroo.

"I would like to know more about the humans of this planet," said Kkrask. "I would," he hesitated, searching for the right word. "Be... grateful if you would assist me."

"Oh, aye?" said Doctaroo sceptically. "Well you're not gonna learn much with me stuck in here, are you?"

"Then we shall return to the surface and you can show me."

"But I'm not from this time, pet. I come from the future," protested Doctaroo.

"Indeed," said Kkrask. "That poses no problem. "My people had mastered the art of temporal mechanics when your ancestors were still crawling around in the mud and slime, eating dirt and banging rocks together." Kkrask said with more than a touch of arrogance to his voice.

Doctaroo's eyes widened. "Gosh," she said with sincerity. "So, relatively recently then?"

Kkrask ignored her. "Even our children have the ability to travel through time."

180

"Alright, show off," muttered Doctaroo.

Robert, who had been keeping an eye out for The Overseer, came up to them. "If we're going to go, we need to go now," he said impatiently. "Mr Wood will have discovered my deception by now."

"Very well." Kkrask took charge. "I can create a portal here," he said tapping at the keys on a device he wore on his wrist. "However, I need destination co-ordinates."

"Ah," said Doctaroo uncertainly. "I'm not very good at maths."

"Your best estimate then."

Robert had gone back to the door, but he now rushed over to them. "He's coming back!" He said urgently. "He'll be here any second!"

"Quickly," urged Kkrask. "The co-ordinates, now!"

"I divvent know!" shouted Doctaroo. "It's about two hundred years or so I think. I don't know any co-ordinates."

Kkrask's fingers tapped furiously at the device. "Very well, I have set it for about two hundred years or so," he said. "I hope it is enough."

"He's *COMING*!" shouted Robert.

Kkrask pressed a blue button on the device and pointed his arm at the wall. A beam of bright white light shot out of a small lens on the side of the device an a familiar glowing portal was projected on the rough stone surface.

"Quickly," said Kkrask hurriedly. "Go through, now!"

Robert and Doctaroo wasted no time and jumped into the whirling, churning vortex. Tapping another button, Kkrask followed.

The Overseer ran into the room just as the vortex closed. He ran up to the wall and beat his fists on it. "No, dammit. No!"

He stood dejectedly facing the spot where his prisoner escaped.

"Oh, pooh!" he moaned.

Chapter Sixteen.

It was a cold cloudless December night in Cherbourg and the harbour was illuminated only by the light of the moon, although this was soon to change.

In an alley behind an abandoned, half demolished warehouse, a tiny pinpoint of light appeared in mid-air. If there had been anybody to witness it, they would have been surprised to see the tiny pinpoint of light grow in size until it formed a glowing white vortex. They would have then been astounded to see two people, a woman and a young man emerge from the vortex and stop breathlessly by a door in the building opposite. The witness would have then been shocked to the core and would probably suffer post-traumatic stress for quite some time at the sight of a large, bipedal creature resembling an anthropomorphic Armadillo. It was quite literally to a person from this time period, the stuff of nightmares.

The vortex faded as quickly as it had appeared. Kkrask looked around him.

"Is this your time, human?" he asked.

"Hang on, let me get my bearings," Doctaroo said, looking around for something she recognised.

Robert was gazing around in wonder. "Is this really the future, miss?" he asked.

"Aye, pet. At least I think it is." She spotted something in the middle distance and began to walk cautiously towards it. Robert and Kkrask followed until they reached the entrance to a small courtyard. Suddenly the door next to them burst open and a dozen or so men dressed in black uniforms, wearing black berets and carrying Sten sub-machine guns ran out and surrounded them. A tall, aristocratic man followed them out. Kkrask growled and reached for the knife on his belt but Doctaroo stopped him. She held up her hands in surrender and indicated that her companions should follow suit. The tall man came over to her. Doctaroo looked up at him.

"Hello, Ian." Doctaroo said with an impish smile. "Fancy meeting *you* here."

The tall man made a sound that was half sigh, half groan and he gestured to his men to lower their weapons.

Doctaroo put down her hands. "Well, if you're here then that means I'm in, oooh," she licked her finger and held it up. "That means I'm in..."

"Trouble, Doctaroo," said the tall man. "As usual!"

Chapter Seventeen.

The genetically engineered lifeform known as ME2 was a remarkable man. His strength, stamina, eyesight, hearing, in fact pretty much everything, was turned up to eleven and it embarrassed him greatly.

He knew he wasn't supposed to feel embarrassed. He wasn't actually supposed to have feelings of any kind. But nevertheless he had them. Whether they were the result of a faulty genome or it was because of something introduced during the foetal stage, he wasn't certain. All he really knew was that he had the same emotional responses as all other human beings, although he was far, far superior to any of them.

At that current moment in time, he was examining the files he had downloaded from Noor's disk using the computer aboard Doctaroo's ship.

Well, part of him was. Around seven percent of his functioning brain's capacity in actual fact. Twelve percent was engaged in monitoring his life support subroutines, nineteen percent was reviewing a recipe he'd come across in a magazine he'd found in the Scotland Yard canteen, twenty eight percent was busy composing an aria he'd dreamt up the night before last and the remaining thirty four percent was studying Beryl's legs which were draped across the chaise longue she happened to be reclining on whilst reading the latest issue of 'Bella' magazine.

They were currently relaxing in the Yard's private spa which was usually for the exclusive use of senior officers only. Brian was swimming lengths in the heated pool, Mr Walsh was having all the day's tension pounded out of his tired muscles by the resident masseuse and Nigel Maule-Ffinch was on his mobile trying to explain exactly what had transpired to the Home Secretary. It wasn't going well.

ME2 stood up, announced to nobody in particular that he was required elsewhere and then left the spa at a run. Maule-Ffinch ended his call and watched Carstairs' doppelgänger go.

"I wonder where he's off to in such a hurry," he mused.

"He's probably gone to tell the Inspector about the files he decrypted off that floppy disk thing," said Beryl without looking up from her magazine. "Hey, did you know that that singer, Ella Gravely has just got engaged to Prince Ludovic of Bavaria?"

"How do you know he's decrypted the disk?" asked Brian, climbing out of the pool and towelling himself off.

"It's pretty obvious, isn't it?" Beryl said turning the page. "Why else would he be running off to speak to the Inspector?"

"How do you know he's going to speak to the Inspector?" asked Maule-Ffinch.

Beryl looked up. "Seriously? Didn't you hear the last thing he said before he left?"

Maule-Ffinch shook his head. Beryl looked at Brian who just shrugged and sat down on a sun lounger.

"You two are bloody useless." Beryl put down the magazine, got up and went over to the small bar area to get a drink.

The door opened and Carstairs entered followed by ME2. Carstairs hopped up on a bar stool next to Beryl while ME2 stood obediently next to him, like a loyal puppy next to its master.

"I hope I'm not interrupting your valuable me-time," he said sarcastically. "But we still have a job to do you know."

Mr Walsh lifted his head up. "We were just waiting for your twin to decipher the information on that disk, mate. There's not much else we can do to help out. Anyway," he said accusatorially. "Shouldn't you be off looking for Doctaroo instead of moaning at us?"

"For your information Mr Walsh, ME2 has decrypted the disk," said Carstairs. Beryl gave Brian a smug grin. Brian ignored her.

"We now know the real purpose of Noor's pipeline," continued Carstairs. "It's a..."

"Never mind that," said Mr Walsh impatiently. "Have you found Doctaroo yet?"

"I'm getting to that!" Carstairs said crossly.

"Well hurry up then," said Mr Walsh.

"I will," said Carstairs. "But first I want to..."

"Come on then," interrupted Mr Walsh. "Spit it out."

"I'm trying to..." spluttered a flustered Carstairs.

"We're waiting," said Mr Walsh.

"If you would stop interrupting me, I w..."

"Look," said Mr Walsh checking his watch. "Time's getting on. We haven't got all day."

Carstairs had had enough. "Enough!" he shouted. "I have had enough!"

(See, I told you he'd had enough.)

"ME2!" Carstairs was visibly shaking. "You tell him."

He poured himself a stiff drink and waited for his double to speak. ME2 cleared his throat.

"The real purpose of Noor's pipeline is to heat water in the pipe to boiling point by diverting geo-thermic energy from the Earth's core into the pipe. Tithe resultant superheated steam will be used to run a series of huge turbines positioned at every former tube station along what used to be called the Circle Line and which will be unveiled by Her Majesty the Queen at a special ceremony this afternoon."

"Is that it?" asked Brian. "Is that all you got from that bloody disk? We already knew that before we started all this!"

"Please," said ME2 calmly. "Let me finish." He smiled benignly at Brian.

"That is the official story. The one Noor sold to the Government and his financial backers. The *genuine* purpose of the pipeline is this," he turned to face the wall behind him. With an audible click, ME2's eyes rolled backwards in his head to reveal twin lenses. These lenses lit up and projected a series of blueprints and schematics onto the white surface of the wall. ME2 continued.

"What you are looking at is a geological survey of the south east of England conducted five years ago, just before work began on the pipeline." ME2 zoomed in on the area surrounding London and its boroughs. "As you can see, there are a number of cracks in the Earth's crust at significant points on the map." He blinked and the picture changed to show which of the cracks were nearest the surface.

"These are of particular interest." He blinked again ant the picture changed to a FLIR image (FLIR – that's Forward Looking Infra-Red – a thermographic camera used by emergency services to locate people trapped in collapsed buildings and tunnels and by bearded loonies hunting cryptozoological myths like Bigfoot and Yeti on certain nature documentaries. There, that saved you a Google. You're welcome).

"These cracks appear to be natural vents, presumably used for venting whatever pressure Mother Nature sees fit to vent."

Carstairs gave a snort. "Goodness me, ME2. You really seem to be embracing the banality of the human condition don't you? Mother Nature indeed." He laughed and poured himself another drink.

ME2 ignored him. "However, the real interest lies in where the cracks originate from. Or perhaps I should say, originate from *now*."

He blinked again and the picture changed to one which showed the blueprint of the pipeline superimposed upon the schematic of the cracks and fissures beneath London. Each fissure, every crack spread downwards from the surface and appeared to join with the pipeline at various points around its circumference.

The lights blinked off and ME2's eyes rolled back to their normal position. He turned to face the others. "It is my estimation that the pipeline is in actuality, a gigantic pressure cooker – to adopt a vernacular more suited to your understanding."

"Cheeky bugger," muttered Beryl. ME2 ignored her.

"I believe that the superheated steam created in the pipeline will not be used for its supposed intended purpose to drive electricity generators. I believe that instead, the steam will be channelled into these cracks and fissures, widening them and subsequently creating shifts in the tectonic plates beneath the city."

Beryl's eyes widened, Brian gave a gasp of horror, Mr Walsh shook his head sadly, Maule-Ffinch buried his head in his hands and Carstairs poured himself another drink.

"Hand on... I mean, hang on," slurred Carstairs, who was rapidly becoming more sloshed by the minute and who was swaying precariously on his stool.

"Hang on," he hiccoughed. "Sorry. Where was I?"

"You were sayin' hang on," said Beryl helpfully.

"Oh yes. Hang on..."

"Spit it out, man!" shouted Mr Walsh, whose patience with the Inspector was wearing thin.

"I'm trying!" Carstairs protested.

194

"Very," replied ME2.

"Look, it's not easy being an Inspector you know." Carstairs said, except he pronounced it Inshpector due to the alcohol coursing through his veins. ME2 looked sadly at his twin.

Drinking on the job, whilst a requisite in the 1970s when Carstairs had joined the force, was kind of frowned upon today. Fortunately, due to his rank and position, Carstairs little error of judgment could be hushed up on the provision that ME2 take his place for a while. Unfortunately, this was something that had recently become a bit of a habit, with ME2's predecessor fulfilling the role on more than one occasion.

"Inspector," said ME2 calmly. "Is your question regarding the generators situated at each former station along the Circle Line?"

It was a guess, obviously. But one ME2 judged to be the correct one given that he had been programmed to think the same way Carstairs did, his designers even duplicating the Inspector's memory engrams in ME2's neural network.

Carstairs was nodding vigorously.

"It is my supposition," continued ME2, "that instead of the proposed turbines, Dr Noor has instead installed devices with which he intends to divert the superheated steam along the aforementioned cracks and fissures."

It is at this point that I would like to point out the following:

ME2 has got it spot on, with just one small but glaring error which will shortly be made clear. However before that happens, I'm afraid we will have to leave our friends to ponder their next move alone as we must first segue to an earlier and bloodier period in Earth's history where we find the erstwhile hero of this tale in the company of a detachment of allied commandos led by one Commander Ian Fleming (yes, that one).

Doctaroo was seated on an upturned bucket and being debriefed by Cmdr. Fleming. Next to her on the floor sat Robert and Kkrask, the big Kkrellem

196

attracting unwanted attention from the soldiers in 30 Assault Unit - the designated title of Fleming's group and which he tended to call his "Red Indians", much to his men's chagrin.

30 Assault Unit was formed to perform diverse and top secret tasks in Europe and beyond during the Second World War. One of which was to undertake covert missions across enemy lines in order to capture any and all intelligence possible in the form of codes, documents, equipment or even high ranking enemy personnel.

"We arrived last night ahead of our main force," explained Fleming. We were all set to make a raid on enemy headquarters when we got word that a special VIP was due to arrive tomorrow morning. Of course, that put the kibosh on our little jaunt and we were told to stay in cover until we could ascertain just who this VIP was."

"Oh right," said Doctaroo. "Well, we won't bother you for very much longer."

"It's no bother Doctaroo. You're welcome to bunk down here with us for as long as you need.

The local Kommandant is pretty lax about nightly patrols, so we're quite safe here for the time being."

Fleming poured boiling water from a saucepan into a several tin mugs. "Only rations I'm afraid," he said, spooning sugar into each mug. "There's not much call for Darjeeling on the front lines." He handed her a mug of tea, then offered another to Robert.

"Thank you, sir," the young man said, gratefully accepting the steaming brew.

Fleming nodded towards Kkrask. "I don't suppose your friend drinks tea, does he?"

Doctaroo shook her head. "I don't know, petal. Why don't you ask him?"

Fleming cleared his throat. "Ah, erm..." he raised an eyebrow at Doctaroo.

"It's Kkrask, pet," she whispered, leaning forward.

"Right. Yes. Well then Mr Kkrask," he said breezily. "Would you care for a cuppa?"

The Kkrellem shook his head slowly. "No, thank you," he said. "I have never acquired the taste for it. However, I do have a liking for the beverage called Kkokkakkolla."

Fleming looked blankly at him for a moment. "No, sorry. Far too many kays in that for me, old chap."

Doctaroo patted him on the arm. "I think he means Coca Cola," she said. "But I can't be certain."

"Oh, right." Fleming said. "Well I'm afraid I can't help you there, old bean. We'll have to hang on until the Yanks arrive for some of that stuff."

Kkrask nodded sadly. "I have only tasted it once," he said reverently, his mouth watering at the memory. "Before I was assigned to the mine at Killingworth. It is a flavour I shall never forget."

"Hmm," said Fleming disdainfully, adding a sixth spoonful of sugar to his mug before stirring and sipping its contents. He grimaced and spooned in a seventh.

"Can't stand the stuff myself. Far too sweet and sickly."

"So who's this VIP you're expecting then Ian?" said Doctaroo.

"Not sure actually. All we were told was that he was coming to take charge of a certain artefact that the Kommandant had locked away in his safe."

Fleming took a deep gulp of tea. "Naturally, we took it upon ourselves to liberate said artefact before the chappie arrives."

He got up and went over to a pile of ammunition boxes and selected one from the top. He carried it back and placed it on the ground in front of Doctaroo.

"We found this, amongst other things of course." He opened the box and took out a heavy diamond necklace.

"Belonged to the Empress Josephine apparently. There were several items that had been looted from the royal palace at Versailles, this was one of them."

Doctaroo peered into the box. "Ooh, what's that?" she asked.

Fleming reached in and removed a heavy gold statuette. "Interesting thing isn't it? Appears to be a cow of some kind. Belonged to Napoleon Bonaparte."

"It's not a cow," said Robert.

"Really?" said Fleming. "What is it then?"

"It's a gnu," said Doctaroo.

Chapter Eighteen.

Henry was bored. He had watched the rugby, eaten the nachos and drank the beer. He lay on the designer leather sofa and played Sudoku on his phone. A few minutes later, having solved even the most difficult puzzle, Henry was bored again.

An intellect such as his needed constant stimulation, he thought. It wouldn't do to be cooped up in Noor's office while the doctor and his earlier aspect got to have all the fun. He lay there for a while just staring at the ceiling and wondering why he couldn't remember events as they occurred to his former self. Must be something to do with his proximity to Kkrellem temporal technology, he thought. The sooner he did away with them, the better. Until then, he decided, he would go out and have a little fun.

He got up and looked around for a set of keys in case he needed to let himself back in before the next day's festivities. He checked cupboards and drawers with no luck and he was about to give up and just go out anyway, when he stumbled upon a floor safe hidden beneath a potted aspidistra.

Henry toyed with the keypad for a while, tapping in numbers at random, none of which yielded any results. He was about to call it a day and revert back to his original plan of going out and raising hell, when he noticed a framed photograph on the wall above.

He got to his feet and examined it closely. The picture was of Noor, taken at the dedication ceremony for the pipeline. He noticed the date. No, it couldn't be. Was Noor that obvious? Henry knelt down and tapped the eight figure number into the keypad. There was a muffled click and the safe door opened. With a satisfied chuckle, Henry rooted through the safe's contents. There was the usual wad of cash, some gold sovereigns, a gun, some docu...

Hang on, he thought. Go back a little. He reached in and took out a SIG Sauer P226. He turned it over in his hands and nodded to himself. Nice, he thought, checking the clip. It was loaded. He thumbed off the safety, pointed it at the television and looked down the barrel. He took a breath, held it and squeezed the trigger.

Laughing at the thunderous crack from the weapon and the resultant nine millimetre hole that appeared in the centre of the screen, Henry dropped the gun back into the safe. The SIG was fun, but nowhere near as fun as his own weapon. He grabbed the money and made for the door, pausing only to check his appearance in the full length mirror on the wall. Satisfied that he looked irresistible, Henry opened the front door and left, slamming it shut behind him.

Had he waited a further five minutes, he would have noticed that the edge of the mirror had begun to glow.

In 1944, Commander Fleming, his commandos, Doctaroo, Robert and Kkrask hunkered down behind a stone wall that ran alongside the road leading into Cherbourg. Fleming had received an intelligence report that the expected VIP would be arriving at midnight, so he had rallied his men and they had made their way out of the town to where they now lay in ambush for the VIP's car.

Doctaroo and her companions had been brought along partly for their protection, but mainly because Fleming didn't trust Doctaroo with his equipment.

One of Fleming's men had been sent to reconnoitre the car's intended route for signs of enemy activity and he now returned with the news that the VIP was on their way, escorted by two Sd.Kfz 222 Leichter Panzerspähwagen armoured vehicles, while the VIP's own transport was a modified Mercedes-Benz W31 staff car.

Fleming checked with one of the Sappers that they had enough explosive to deal with the armoured cars, then he ordered the two men to hide on opposite sides of the road, each with a rucksack filled with containers of Amatol and appropriate detonators. The plan was to deal with the Panzerspähwagens first, then capture the staff car with its oh so very important passenger.

Hearing the sound of approaching engines, Fleming gave the order and his men moved into position.

As the small convoy rounded the bend, the Sappers sprang into action, each throwing their bag of explosives into the open hatches of the armoured cars either side of the Mercedes.

As each bag of Amatol detonated, the armoured car veered across the road, crashing over the verge and down the hill before crashing onto the rocks below.

The staff car sped up, but Fleming's men were ready for it. They emerged from hiding and sprayed the front of the car with bullets which pinged off the heavy armoured steel body panels. One stray shot caught the driver through the neck and he slumped over the wheel. The car swerved and crashed into the wall. Fleming and his men ran to surround it with their weapons drawn.

Doctaroo and Robert peered cautiously over the top of the wall, while Kkrask lay against it, his eyes closed. For a second, Doctaroo worried that he had caught a stray bullet, but then he began to snore loudly.

The rear door of the Mercedes opened slowly and a hand emerged waving a white handkerchief. The hand was followed by an arm, which was in turn followed by a head and a body dressed in black trousers, double-breasted field-grey coat, white shirt and black tie. He wore a golden Nationalsozialistische Deutsche Arbeiterpartei badge on the left side of his chest and an Iron Cross below it. Topping and tailing his ensemble was the peaked officer's cap of the Wehrmacht and leather jackboots.

Fleming let out a gasp of horror, surprise and elation. He was expecting someone important, but never in his life had he expected *him!*

Admittedly, he looked somewhat different to his photographs, Fleming hadn't expected the mutton chop whiskers for a start, but the toothbrush moustache was a dead giveaway. He turned to

Doctaroo who was staring at the newcomer with an expression of fear, dread and disappointment.

"Doctaroo," said Fleming as proudly as he would show off a new-born child to his family and friends. "May I introduce the Fuhrer himself, Adolf bloody Hit..."

"I know who he is," she said bitterly. "Even wearing that silly fake moustache, I can tell who he is. That's Charlie Chaplin."

Dr Noor was happily rubbing shoulders with some of the world's most powerful people. There were world leaders, royalty, billionaire entrepreneurs like himself and of course, Kylie. Ah, Kylie. If she only knew how the young Johar had gazed upon her beauteous countenance as she learned the basics of car mechanics before meeting Scott and Mike at Daphne's coffee shop for a milkshake after school, or just hanging around with Jane at Mrs Mangel's house. The usually ice cool Noor was reduced to a stammering, shaking fanboy when he finally plucked up the courage to introduce himself. When he discovered that the fragrant Ms Minogue had actually heard of him and his achievements, it came as such a surprise that Noor was for perhaps the only time in his life, rendered utterly speechless. When she leaned forward and kissed him on the cheek, Noor's carefully crafted air of nonchalant superiority gave up and went off to bother somebody else, leaving the poor man to deal with Richard Branson and that annoying Musk person without the usual verbal armoury he usually relied on. Fortunately, just as Branson and Musk descended on him, Noor's phone rang. He answered it quickly, holding up a finger to halt the approaching businessmen.

"Hello?" he asked, making a 'sorry but what can I do, I have to take this" kind of gesture. Branson and Musk moved off to mingle with the other guests.

"Is that you, Johar?" asked an Australian voice. Noor confirmed that it was.

"Aww, bonzer mate!" the voice continued. "Have a guess where *I* am."

"Is that you, Henry?" asked Noor, a touch of annoyance creeping into his voice.

"Sure is mate. I bet you can't guess what I'm doing either." There came the sound of raucous laughter, then Henry's muffled voice telling whoever he was with to 'pipe down'.

"You're supposed to be at my apartment," Noor hissed. "Where the hell are you?"

"Soho," came the one word reply.

"Soho? What the bloody hell are you doing in Soho?"

There was more laughter. "I'm having a *par-tay*!"

Noor ended the call and angrily dialled Renifler's number. There was a click and the Frenchman answered.

"Oui?"

"Henry's in Soho. Go find him and take him back to the apartment."

Renifler sighed dramatically. "Merde," he grunted. "I cannot leave the control centre, M'sieur. We have just begun to draw power to the system

210

from the Kkrellem vessel, it is a critical point in the operation."

"What about the Kkrellem the Overseer sent through to oversee things?" asked Noor impatiently. "Can't he be left in charge while you go and get that annoying prick from whatever backstreet boozer he's ended up in?"

There was a moment's silence, then Renifler cleared his throat. "Ah, erm, that might be a problem M'sieur," he said slowly. "The Kkrellem supervisor is unable to take charge on account of him being ever so slightly dead."

Noor closed his eyes and rubbed his temple with his free hand. He was beginning to feel the first tiny signs of one hell of a migraine coming on.

"Ever so slightly dead?" he repeated. "What have you done this time?"

"It was a situation beyond my control, M'sieur. My gun went off unexpectedly when I was pointing it at his head and his brains were inadvertently blown out by a stray bullet or six."

"You know, Renifler. I'm constantly surprised and amazed at the lengths you go to try

211

and make your acts of cold blooded murder sound like unintentional accidents." Noor sounded weary. "That American senator last year, for example. The one who supposedly died in a freak juicing mishap?"

"Ah, Oui. Senator Callaghan," said Renifler sadly. "Such a shame, but that's what happens if you don't read the instruction manual properly."

"He was found hanging by the flex in his hall from the upstairs bannister rail with an orange in his mouth and a pineapple up his bottom!" Noor whispered fiercely. "How the hell was that a bloody juicing mishap?"

If it is possible to shrug noncommittally over the phone, then that's what Renifler did. Noor made his displeasure clear.

"Look, I don't care who you get to supervise the pipeline, I want you to go get McLachlan and take him back to the flat, okay? The man's a bloody liability and I don't want him ruining everything we've worked for." Noor forced himself to calm down. "Once The Overseer arrives from 1819, then Henry is his responsibility. He can deal with him."

212

"Very well, M'sieur. I will sort something out for you."

"Good. Oh and Renifler?" Noor said coldly.

"Oui, M'sieur?" the Frenchman asked.

"I want you to take good care of Mr McLachlan. See that some harm comes to him."

Doctaroo sat on her bucket and stared at Fleming's prisoner. After much arguing and shouting, she had been persuaded to accept that the prisoner was not the famous actor Charlie Chaplin, but was instead the erstwhile Chancellor of Germany. However, she was not fully convinced of this. Partly because he didn't speak a word of German, partly because of his painfully obviously false moustache, but mostly because she was now absolutely certain that he was, in fact, The Overseer in disguise.

How did she know this, you ask? Was it her superior detective skills, honed to perfection by several lifetimes? Was it her lightning fast powers of deduction, said to rival those of the great Sherlock

Holmes himself? Was it her computer-like mind, sharp as a steel trap?

No. Actually it was because he had spent the past hour telling her who he was and finally, thank the gods, finally she had shut up and listened.

"So," she said carefully, not wanting to get anything wrong. "You're not Charlie Chaplin then?"

"No," said The Overseer wearily, leaning back against the wall and gently banging the back of his head on the stone surface.

"But you're also not this Hitler bloke either?" Her forehead creased in concentration.

"That's correct." The Overseer said quietly.

"And you're definitely not that bloke from Sparks?"

The Overseer shook his head.

Doctaroo stared at him for a second, then shook her head and just shrugged at her incomprehension at the situation.

"In that case," she said, bewildered. "I haven't the foggiest."

The Overseer let out a cry so filled with frustration that Fleming and his men actually felt sorry for the person they took to be the most evil man who ever lived.

"It's simple, you blundering, obtuse simpleton!" he shouted. "I'm The Overseer! Look," he removed his stuck on moustache. "See? It's fake. Look at me, for crying out loud! You were with me in 1819 only a few hours ago!"

Doctaroo blinked several times. "Well, I suppose you do look a *bit* like him," she said. "In the right light you'd be a ringer for him."

The Overseer turned to Fleming. "Please, Commander. Put me up against a wall and shoot me. *Anything* is preferable to having to talk to this woman for even a minute longer."

"Just you be quiet, Fritz," said Fleming. "You're coming back to Blighty with me for questioning. Afterwards, if you're lucky, it'll be the firing squad."

"And if I'm *unlucky*?" asked The Overseer, already dreading the answer.

Fleming grinned and lit a cigarette. "We'll lock you up with *her*."

Chapter Nineteen.

Henry staggered from the nightclub and grabbed hold of a handy lamppost. One of the doormen asked if he was okay and if he wanted him to hail a cab for him. Henry declined with a smile and bidding both the doormen a cheery goodnight, staggered off down the road in search of a kebab shop.

Arriving at a late night takeaway on Oxford Street after a slight detour to a television post-production facilities house doorway on Wardour Street, where he had relieved himself of some of the lager he had imbibed earlier, Henry ordered a large doner kebab with extra onion and chilli sauce. He left the takeaway in good spirits and set off up the road in roughly the direction of Noor's apartment. He passed a homeless guy squatting in the same doorway he had watered ten minutes age.

Feelings of both sympathy and guilt vied for attention in his conscious mind.

Eventually, sympathy won out and Henry crossed the street to speak to the man.

"G'day mate. How're you doing?"

"Bugger off," said the man, heavily edited for content.

"Aww, don't be like that." Henry proffered the kebab. "Here, get this down your neck, you look like you need it more than me."

The man took the kebab from him and opened the polystyrene box.

"Is the pitta bread gluten free?" he asked suspiciously. Henry shrugged.

"No idea mate."

The man examined the pitta's contents, then thrust it angrily into Henry' hands. "I'm a flipping vegan!" he shouted PG-thirteenedly.

"Alright mate, keep your shirts on. I'm only trying to help." Henry was slightly taken aback by the man's attitude.

"Yeah," said the man. "That's what they all say. Bloody do-gooders always interfering when they're not wanted. You're as bad as that lot from the Sally Ann, forcing their god awful soup on us. Always sticking their nose into my affairs. Go on," he said forcefully. "Do one."

Henry looked at him for a moment, then removed a small rectangular box from his pocket. It was about the size and shape of a cigarette packet. He held it up so that the man could see it.

"Do you know what this is?" he asked.

"It's a packet of Rothman's King Size."

Henry cursed under his breath and reached into his other pocket. This time the small box was made from an alloy not yet discovered on Earth. It had a push button on one side and a black nozzle on one of the shorter ends.

"How about this then?" asked Henry.

The man shook his head. Henry pointed the end with the nozzle at him.

"This is my T.E.I. That stands for Tissue Expansion Inflator (pat pending)," he explained. "And it works like this..."

Henry pushed the button. The nozzle emitted a narrow beam of purple light which enveloped the homeless man. He screamed as his body began to inflate like a balloon. Bones cracked, his skin burst like an overcooked sausage, then he exploded.

The resultant slurry of blood, flesh and bone was contained within the purple bubble created by the T.E.I, then with a slurp and a gurgle, it was dehydrated and compressed into a small red cube that Henry picked up and dropped into a nearby bin.

"Can't stand bloody vegans," he said, then he took a mouthful of kebab and set off for Noor's apartment.

"Are you completely bonkers?" asked Mr Walsh once Brian had outlined his plan. "That'll never work. Not in a month of Sundays."

They were sitting on a wall outside Scotland Yard. Beryl was filing her nails and intermittently drinking from a carton of pineapple juice, Mr Walsh was nursing a fresh espresso from the canteen and Brian was finishing his eighth can of Red Bull (other energy drinks are available. Personally, I'd rather have a bottle of flavoured spring water, but each to their own, eh?).

They had been discussing what they were going to do to get Doctaroo back and Brian, his brain firing on all four cylinders at once as opposed to the usual two and a bit, had come up with a plan so cunning and foolhardy and yet also daring in its simplicity.

Brian opened his mouth to speak, but Beryl interrupted him.

"Shush, here comes Nigel."

Maule-Ffinch was walking down the steps to join them. His forehead was creased in a frown and his lips were set firmly against one another.

"I thought I'd find you out here," he said. "Carstairs reckons you're plotting something."

The three friends said nothing.

"Well?" continued Maule-Ffinch. "Are you?"

Brian stepped forward, chin raised, pupils the size of pin pricks.

"So what if we are?" he said defiantly. "What are you gonna do about it?"

Maule-Ffinch met his icy glare with one of his own.

"I'm going to join you, of course!" he exclaimed. "Carstairs is three sheets to the wind and I'd trust that ME2 robot thing about as far as I could comfortably throw a three tonne lorry. Besides, I'd like to know what happened to Doctaroo too."

Mr Walsh patted him heartily on the back. "Well said, Nigel. Glad you're on *our* side."

"Well, who else's side *would* I be on?" said Maule-Ffinch with a smile. "I feel terrible about what's been happening. After all, I got you into this in the first place."

"Yeah, you did, divvy." Beryl pointed at Maule-Ffinch with her nail file. "If it wasn't for you dragging us here from Hyde Park we'd be havin' dinner at the Dorchester by now."

Maule-Ffinch wrung his hands in contrition. "Believe me, I feel awfully guilty about the whole bally mess. If it's any consolation, I promise that when this is over, I'll take you all to dinner at the Ritz. My treat."

Beryl calmed down a bit and went back to her manicuring. "You'd better." One final parting shot that had the desired effect of making Maule-Ffinch go as red as a beetroot.

"So, what are we going to do?" Brian asked. Mr Walsh puffed out his cheeks.

"Dunno, mate. You're the one with the degree."

Brian rolled his eyes. "I've already told you, I haven't passed yet. Besides, it's an art degree. Unless you want me to paint you a pretty picture of Dr Noor and his assorted minions then I'm hardly going to be of use, am I?"

Maule-Ffinch cleared his throat. "Erm, I have degrees in physics and applied mathematics from Keble College Oxford. Not much I know,

Father wanted me to attend Magdalen his alma mater but I flunked the entry exam. Only eighty nine percent you see. Anyway, what I'm saying in a roundabout way is, well, perhaps I may be of assistance?"

Mr Walsh looked at Brian who in turn looked at Beryl. Beryl looked at Maule-Ffinch who looked back at Mr Walsh. Once they had established who was looking at whom, Mr Walsh spoke.

"Yeah, well. Sounds good to me, eh Brian?"

"Oh yeah, definitely," he said, nodding at Beryl.

"What do you think?"

She glanced over at Maule-Ffinch. "Yeah, I suppose so," she said, half smiling. "What we really need though is someone with a bit of clout, you know? Someone who knows someone high up in, say, the government or somethin."

Maule-Ffinch's eyes lit up. "Gosh," he said with building excitement. "I know the bally Home Secretary! Would *he* do?"

"Oh, gosh Nigel," said Beryl with heavy sarcasm. "Do yer really? Wow, isn't *that* lucky, Mr Walsh? Nigel knows the Home Secretary."

Both Mr Walsh and Brian covered their mouths to hide a smile. Maule-Ffinch took out his mobile.

"Should I give him a call now, do you think? Would that be prudent?"

Beryl threw her empty juice carton at him. "Get on with it, soft lad."

Nigel Maule-Ffinch dialled the number he had been told only to call in the most extreme and dire emergency. Well, he thought as the receiver at the other end was picked up, if this didn't count as an extreme and dire emergency then he was buggered if he knew what did.

In Noor's apartment, seconds after Henry had left, the surface of the full length mirror hung on the wall opposite the bathroom door, started to glow. The light intensified in strength and eventually became a whirling, swirling vortex of a myriad tones and colours that ran from one end of the visible spectrum to the other. Far in the distance, four minute figures appeared and grew steadily bigger as though moving closer to the event horizon of the vortex.

As one, the four figures emerged into corporeal space and leapt from the mirror, tumbling to the floor. The first to jump to his feet, The Overseer ran into the living room and frantically looked around for something - anything - to use as a weapon.

His gaze was drawn to the open safe in the floor and in particular, the SIG Sauer P226 sticking up out of it.

Realising that their prisoner had escaped, Robert and Doctaroo also ran into the living room only to be greeted by The Overseer pointing the gun at them. Behind them in the hall, they could hear muffled grunts and shouting as Kkrask struggled to extricate himself from the towel rail he'd crashed into after falling into the bathroom from the mirror vortex.

"Don't come in Kkrask, he's got a gun," warned Doctaroo.

"Shut up!" The Overseer exclaimed. "What are you doing for goodness sake? I've got a gun!"

"Aye, I know," said Doctaroo helpfully. "An' I'm just warning my friend about it."

"Well, stop it!" said The Overseer. "You're not supposed to warn people that I've got a gun."

Doctaroo shook her head. "Well that's a bit daft. How's he goin' to know not to come in if I divvent warn him about it?"

"But that's not how it works!" The Overseer was almost ready to tear his hair out in frustration. He really didn't know why he let her get to him like this. "You're all supposed to come in together," he said through gritted teeth. "That way I can capture you."

"Oh come on," said Doctaroo. "That makes *no* sense at all. The last thing we want is to let you capture us."

"I *know* that!" said The Overseer. "But how else am I going to oversee all of you?"

Robert started laughing. "Hahaha," he chortled. *"Oversee!* And you're called The Overseer! Oh that's funny. Do you get it, Miss?"

"Aye pet," said Doctaroo. "An' it wasn't funny the last time I heard it either.

Several hours and many pints later, Henry arrived back at the flat. He had been carried to a waiting taxi outside the club by two friendly doormen, who he tipped generously, hugged and given his phone number to saying that he could use two guys like them for a job he had planned and did they have their own photon cannons. The doormen humoured Henry and bundled him into the back of the cab.

Eventually, once he remembered where Noor lived, he arrived back at the flat where he handed the driver a wad of noted and bade him goodnight. He staggered in and rode the lift up to Noor's floor. He struggled with the keys for a moment, then finally managed to get the key in the lock and having successfully turned it, Henry staggered into the apartment and put the bag he was carrying onto the floor by the kitchen.

He was surprised to see a two metre tall Kkrellem warrior checking his face in the bathroom mirror, he was staggered to see Doctaroo in the open doorway of the living room and he was completely stunned at the sight of the figure of his earlier aspect pointing the gun he'd discovered in the safe, in his general direction.

Henry stood for a moment, not knowing what to do next. After a second or two, he turned, picked up the bag, went into the kitchen and sat down at the table. He decided to wait for a while to make sure that they weren't just figments of his imagination.

To aid him in this, Henry removed a six pack of Special Brew from the plastic carrier bag. He opened it with one hand and then downed the entire can in one go.

"Look," he shouted. I'm not completely certain that your real or just hallucinations brought on by too many Jägerbombs. So if you would be so

228

kind as to let me know at some point, I'd be extremely grateful."

Doctaroo shouted from the living room.

"WooOOOoooooo... I'm the ghost of Christmas past..."

The Overseer sniggered at this, then recovered and said rather haughtily,

"If you don't mind, Doctaroo. I'd rather you didn't wind up my future persona."

"You're just jealous because you didn't think of it first."

As this was closer to the truth than The Overseer would have preferred to say, he did the sensible thing and ignored her. Instead he called out to Henry.

"Don't listen to her Henry," he began, then something about the way Doctaroo was looking at him must have triggered something inside because the next thing he found himself saying was:

"I am the ghost of Christmas present, woooOOOooo..."

Both he and Doctaroo had a sudden fit of the giggles. Henry poked his head around the door frame.

"Hello," he said. "You're supposed to be dead," he pointed at Doctaroo, then at his predecessor. "You were supposed to have killed her. Fat lot of good *you* were."

The Overseer frowned. "There were circumstances beyond my control. I didn't foresee my assistant's betrayal or that of a treacherous Kkrellem. Plus, let's face it, if she fell into a barrel of horse manure she'd come up smelling of bloody roses!"

Doctaroo smiled modestly. She opened her mouth to speak when suddenly the front door slammed open and hit the wall with a bang. In the doorway was framed the tall, skinny figure of Renifler who stalked towards them. He walked past the kitchen, past the bathroom where Kkrask was tasting the contents of Noor's bathroom cabinet and was currently knocking back a bottle of minty fresh mouthwash.

In his hands, Renifler carried a pair of Beretta 93R machine pistols which he raised and pointed at Doctaroo, who ran for cover behind The Overseer.

"I am pleased you returned, M'sieur." Renifler said to Henry. "It makes finding you so much easier."

"Hey," said Henry with a cheerful smile. "Never let it be said that I don't try to accommodate my friends, mate."

"Indeed." Renifler said grimly. "Unfortunately, we are not friends. However, there is a bright side to this, it makes killing you so very much easier." He raised one of the Berettas.

"Any final words, M'sieur?"

Henry raised both hands in surrender. "Nah, nothing springs to mind."

Renifler's finger tightened on the trigger. There was a loud bang and Renifler dropped to the floor, a 9mm hole drilled neatly through the centre of his forehead a wisp of smoke drifting upwards from it in a lazy ribbon.

"Hey, nice shot mate!" Henry exclaimed in delight.

The Overseer blew down the barrel of the SIG he'd taken from the safe.

"I *aim* to please," he punned dreadfully. Doctaroo groaned and came out of hiding behind him. Robert had fainted, collapsing onto a handy nearby sofa. In the bathroom, Kkrask had moved on from the mouthwash and was now swigging from a bottle he had found in the cupboard.

Henry bent to examine Renifler's body. "This Guy worked for Dr Noor," he said rooting through his pockets. "He's his go-to guy if he wants something done that he normally wouldn't want to soil his hands with." He stopped suddenly and exclaimed. "That's odd!"

The Overseer joined him. Both men examined the body thoroughly from head to toes. The Overseer beckoned Doctaroo over.

"Come and have a look at this," he said.

Doctaroo came over cautiously. "Oh, no. He isn't pierced in the unmentionables, or got a tattoo on his belly of an arrow pointing down and the words 'Get it here' above it, has he?"

The Overseer frowned ever so slightly. "Well, yes. But that's not what I want you to see."

"Does he have a Prince Albert?" Doctaroo brightened a little.

Henry looked at her, open mouthed.

"What the hell is *wrong* with you?" he asked incredulously. "We're you dropped on your head as a baby or something?"

"Aye, how did you know?" she asked, crouching down next to the body. She gave Renifler the once over.

"I've never seen anything like it," said The Overseer. He looked at Henry. "Have you?"

"I'm you, you idiot. Of course I haven't." Henry replied scathingly.

"Yes, but you're a later model, you div. you've lived longer than me." The Overseer punched him on the arm. He turned to Doctaroo. "Is it suicide or murder if you shoot your future self in the head?" he asked.

"Just try it, cobber." Henry replied. "I might just shoot *you* first!"

"But then you wouldn't exist, would you? So how would you be around to shoot me?"

Doctaroo covered her ears. "Oh, don't get into all that time travel paradox stuff. It gives me a headache."

"Well, what do you think of this then?" He kicked Renifler's body. "Seen anything like it before?"

"Aye," nodded Doctaroo. "In DCI Carstairs' Office at Scotland Yard."

"What?" said The Overseer.

"It's called a biological genetic person thingy, or something."

"A genetically engineered artificial lifeform?" asked The Overseer. "You mean they actually managed to get those things working?"

He calls it "ME2," said Henry slapping his forehead with a groan. "I was wrong mate. I *have* seen this before."

"It's all a bit creepy if you ask me," said Doctaroo.

234

Henry stood up and began pacing up and down. "Okay, we now know that Noor has access to the same tech as Carstairs," he muttered. "Question is, what came first, the chicken or the egg?"

"The chicken!" Doctaroo said decisively. "No, the egg. No, hang on, it's the chicken. No, no it's definitely the egg." She scratched her chin. "It could be the chicken though. Or the egg."

"What the hell are you wittering on about?" demanded The Overseer.

"What came first," she said by way of an explanation. "It's got t' be one of them. Or it could be neither of them, ahhHHHhhh." She winked knowingly.

Both Overseers stared incredulously at her, as though she'd suddenly sprouted wings and a tail and declared herself to be the Archbishop of Canterbury. Again.

Henry addressed his predecessor. "Right, let's assume for arguments sake that both Noor and Carstairs have access to the same tech. Did Noor steal it from the Met or was it the other way round?"

"That's if you assume it was stolen," chimed in Doctaroo. "How do we know that they didn't just share it in the first place?"

"Oh do be quiet Doctaroo, the grown-ups are talking," sighed The Overseer.

Henry held up a hand. "No, hang on mate," he said. "I reckon she might just have a point."

"WHAT???" shouted both The Overseer and Doctaroo simultaneously. They stared at each other in amazement.

"Ooh, I feel right queer," she said as she put a hand to her head. "I think I need a lie down."

The Overseer was too shocked to speak. He gestured for Henry to continue.

"Well, think about it. The technology is far too advanced for the Metropolitan Police to have come up with," he said. "Really only a billionaire genius with access to alien tech and the funds to develop it, could have. So what if Noor and Carstairs *are working together*?"

"The double crossing little fu..." began The Overseer. Henry interrupted him.

"I know, right?"

His predecessor shook his head ruefully. "I blame myself. But it's hard to *oversee* everything from two hundred years in the past."

Henry chuckled. "Heh heh heh, that never gets old."

"What doesn't?" asked Doctaroo. "I still don't get it."

The Overseer opened his mouth to explain, but Henry shook his head and put his hand on his arm. "Don't bother, mate. It's not worth it."

Kkrask wandered in from the bathroom. "The food in this house is very strange," he said. "I ate some bizarre fruit that tasted like wax but which made foam in my mouth. And as for the alcoholic beverages. What kind of drink *is* this Old Spice?"

Chapter Twenty

Nigel Maule-Ffinch, Mr Walsh, Brian and a reluctant Beryl had taken a taxi to Blackfriars station. Maule-Ffinch had spent the journey talking on his mobile to his superior at the Home Office and had managed to persuade the Home Secretary to send a platoon of Royal Marines to meet them on Blackfriars Bridge.

Mr Walsh sat quietly, just looking out the window at all the people innocently going about their business, completely unaware of the possible threat to their lives from the pipeline just beneath the surface of the roads and pavements upon which they travelled.

Brian was munching on a Mars bar, claiming it helped him centre his mind for the struggle that lay ahead.

Beryl was complaining about a cracked nail and scowling her displeasure at the bumps in the road at which the taxi driver seemed deliberately to be aiming the cab.

"I swear if he hits one more speed bump at forty miles an hour, then I'm gonna swing for him," she stated forcefully.

As they neared the station, Maule-Ffinch leaned forward. "Here will do, driver."

The cab pulled over and the four companions got out. Maule-Ffinch thrust a handful of notes at the driver and waited for the change. Brian began walking towards the station's entrance only to be stopped by an armed police officer. Maule-Ffinch, Beryl and Mr Walsh hurried over to join him. Maule-Ffinch showed the officer his Home Office pass and the constable reluctantly let them pass. Inside the ticket hall, they were met by an army lieutenant who handed out Kevlar body armour to each of them.

"Put these on please," said the lieutenant. He took them over to a hastily put together command centre - really just a table, a whiteboard and a few sandbags - and showed them a map of Noor's underground facility.

"The primary command centre is here," he said pointing a massive hexagonal shape under the river. "He pointed to a smaller hexagon. Secondary control is here, crew quarters here and the main turbine is here," he indicated other sections of the map.

Maule-Ffinch tapped the bigger hexagon. "Is Noor there?"

"Yes," said the lieutenant. He arrived about ten minutes ago."

"And you let him in?" asked Beryl incredulously. "Fat lot of good you lot are."

Maule-Ffinch held up a hand. "At least we're know where he is, Beryl. This way we can keep a close eye on things."

"Shouldn't we be going down there to stop him then?" asked Mr Walsh.

"Yeah," said Brian. "Should we go and get a ticket or something?"

Beryl stared at him. "Are you mental?" she asked. "They don't do tickets anymore, they use cockle cards now."

"I think you mean Oyster cards," interrupted Mr Walsh.

"Cockles, oysters, I knew it was some kind of seafood."

Maule-Ffinch knocked for attention on the table. The three friends stopped talking and turn to look at the surprisingly tense civil servant.

"Thank you," he said. "For one thing, this is no longer a functioning tube station and for another, we're not doing anything until Doctaroo arrives."

Beryl, Mr Walsh and Brian looked at each other and then back at Maule-Ffinch. For a moment they were silent, then in unison they cried:

"You're havin' a laugh!"

For probably the first time in their lives, Doctaroo and The Overseer had decided to work together. They had carried the double of Renifler into Noor's bedroom and dumped it on the bed. Seated around the kitchen table, they had discussed their next move should be to confront Noor at Blackfriars station. Doctaroo started to laugh.

"What's so funny?" asked Henry.

"Nothing," she said bitterly. "That's the trouble. You two are giving it loads about stopping this Noor gadgie now that he's not working from your playbook, but a few hours earlier you were planning to cause floods and earthquakes and goodness knows what. It's a tad hypocritical, don't you think?"

Henry and The Overseer looked at each other, then back at her.

"No," said Henry.

"Not at all," said The Overseer.

"The thing is," said Henry standing up and spreading his arms wide. He began to walk around the kitchen, Doctaroo having to duck at least twice to avoid being slapped.

"The thing you really, *really* have to remember, is that I'm..."

"We're," said The Overseer.

"...a villain. A bad guy. A ne'er do well. *Everything* I do..."

"We do," his predecessor muttered.

"...is entirely for *my*..."

"Our," said the older version with a sigh.

"...own benefit. D'you see?"

Kkrask rose from a chair he was far too big for and towered menacingly over Henry.

"We must go now!" he insisted. "My people have no knowledge of what the Noor has planned. They may be in danger."

"Aye," said Doctaroo. "And the thousands of people..."

"Millions," interrupted The Overseer.

"What?" asked Doctaroo.

"The millions of people, not thousands."

"Does it really matter?" She stood up and put her hands on her hips.

"Well, to the millions of people in London, yes. I think it just might." The Overseer rose from his chair. "But instead of standing here arguing about it, perhaps we might be of more help to them by popping along to Blackfriars and stopping Noor? Possibly? Hmm?"

"What about him?" asked Henry pointing at Kkrask. "He's not exactly inconspicuous."

"Aye," said Doctaroo. "You don't often see eight foot tall giant armoured armadillos in West Kensington these days."

"Or at all," said Henry.

The Overseer went out into the hall and looked around. He spotted a door next to the mirror on the other side of the bathroom.

"There," he said striding over to it. "A closet. There might be an overcoat or something he could wear to disguise his, um, armadilloness."

He reached out and turned the door handle, pulling it towards him. It swung open and The Overseer screamed like a teenage girl watching a horror movie.

The others dashed to see what was wrong and were just in time to see The Overseer back away as a horribly mutilated body fell towards him. It hit

244

the tiled floor with a slap and they staggered back in alarm.

Henry stepped forward to see who it used to be.

"I don't believe it."

Doctaroo took a look and gave a gasp and covered her mouth with a hand.

"It can't be," she said.

Robert peered around Kkrask's shoulder. "Who is it?" he asked curiously.

"The last person I expected to see dumped in a cupboard, that's for sure," said Henry.

"Aye," said the young engineer. "*But who is it?*"

The body in the cupboard was none other than Dr Johar Noor.

ME2 had carried an unconscious Carstairs back to his office where he gently laid him on the couch. He made sure that there was no chance he would choke if he vomited, then went over to the desk. He opened a drawer and removed the remote control that Carstairs had used earlier and slipped it into his pocket. Then he reached into another drawer and took out Carstairs' Glock. He checked that it was loaded, then pushed it into the waistband of his trousers behind him and covered it with his jacket.

ME2 then went over to the alcove in which he 'rested' when not in use. He reached in and pressed a button at the back of the door jamb and the back panel of the alcove slid up to reveal a full length mirror. He pushed back his left sleeve to reveal a Kkrellem time travel cuff strapped to his wrist. He pressed some controls and activated the temporal vortex.

The edges of the mirror began to glow.

After dumping the body of Dr Noor next to the replica of Renifler, Doctaroo and her party, including Robert and an uncomfortable Kkrask dressed in a black raincoat several sizes too small, quietly left the apartment and set off along the road to the nearest tube station.

The Overseer took the lead saying that their best option was to head for the Gloucester Road station.

"Isn't that on the Circle Line though?" asked Doctaroo. "Wasn't it turned into the pipeline?"

"Yes," replied The Overseer. "But the pipeline only runs along one side of the tunnels. We kept the other side free so we could use it for maintenance. There's a single carriage train kept at there for that reason. Now come on!"

They broke into a steady jog along Kensington High Street until they arrived at the closed and locked shutters covering the entrance to the station. The Overseer unlocked the heavy padlock and then both he and Henry pushed up one of the shutters. The Overseer ushered the others into the station's dark interior. Then, pulling a torch from his coat pocket, he shone the beam around until he located the main circuit breaker. He walked over to it and threw the switch. Instantly the station came to life. The lights came on, the escalators began to move and the newly fitted bank of computers where the ticket machines used to be, whirred into action.

"Right," said The Overseer gesturing for the others to follow him. "This way."

He led them down the escalator and onto what remained of one of the platforms. On the track in front of them was what looked like a chopped down version of a London Underground tube train. It was about six metres long with a fully automated drivers cab and six pairs of seats arranged on either side of a narrow gangway.

Henry pressed a button next to the single set of doors and they slid open with a hiss. As they boarded the train, Doctaroo took a last look around and let out a little sigh.

"No," she said softly. "It's just not the same without a busker with a whippet on a string and a badly tuned guitar singing 'Here Comes the Sun'."

Chapter Twenty-One

At Blackfriars, Maule-Ffinch has finally been persuaded to send the army in to storm the control centre. The young lieutenant, who they had learned was called Morris, was giving instructions to a specially selected team of twenty or so men and women who were equipped with the very latest in stealth technology.

Mr Walsh watched their briefing with intense curiosity as Lt Morris briefed them on each piece of equipment they carried. Satisfied that they were ready, Morris set off down the escalator followed by his assault team.

Mr Walsh turned to Maule-Ffinch and tapped him on the arm.

"Excuse me, Nigel," he said. Maule-Ffinch looked up from the map of the facility.

"Yes Mr Walsh?"

Mr Walsh pointed over to where the last of the soldiers led by Lt Morris had just vanished down the escalator to the tunnels.

"Just as a matter of interest, who manufactures that equipment they're using?"

Maule-Ffinch shook his head. "No idea, old chap. Tell you what, I'll ask."

He picked up a two way radio from the table. He thumbed the call button and spoke into the mic.

"Lieutenant?" he called. There was a crackle of static and Morris's voice came over the radio.

"Sir?"

"We were just wondering who manufactures your equipment, over?"

In the tunnel below, Morris checked the tag on one of the packs.

"National Utilities & Technology Services, over," he called back.

"That's Noor's company!" Mr Walsh said in alarm. "We've got to get them back."

Maule-Ffinch gave a short laugh.

"Really Mr Walsh, I'm sure everything will be fine. There's probably nothing to worry about."

"Oh yeah?" said Mr Walsh. "And what if you're wrong? Do you really want to take that chance?"

Maule-Ffinch pursed his lips then thumbed the button on the radio.

"Lieutenant Morris?"

There was a crackle of static, then the distorted sound of Morris's voice came through the speaker.

"Sir?"

"On second thoughts, I've decided to wait a bit longer, so I need you and your team to come back, over."

The static grew louder and Morris's voice seemed more distorted.

"...t recei... you, over?"

Maule-Ffinch frowned. "Sorry, Lieutenant," he said loudly. "Say again please, I didn't quite catch that, over."

The radio hissed and crackled even more loudly now.

"...n't hear... t... you... d, o...er?"

The radio gave an almighty squeal and Maule-Ffinch turned it off and rubbed his ears. Mr Walsh looked at him with concern.

"Nothing to worry about, Nigel?" he said.

Maule-Ffinch drew his lips into a thin, hard line. This didn't bode well, he thought.

The compact tube train sped through the tunnel towards Blackfriars. Inside, the two versions of The Overseer were sitting in two of the front seats talking quietly, while Robert was sat at the back of the carriage gazing in wonder at the various stations as they whizzed past the windows. Occasionally, he would give a small cry of alarm or a gentle laugh at every new sight and sound, or throwing the odd question to Doctaroo regarding where the boiler was for the steam or where the coal was burned to heat the water. When she explained that the engine ran on electricity and not steam, Robert simply shook his head in amazement.

Doctaroo herself was standing by the doors with a sad look on her face. Kkrask was next to her, his head bowed because of the limited height of the carriage.

"Why don't you sit down, pet?" Doctaroo said gently. "It can't be comfortable standing there with your neck all bent down like that."

Kkrask shook his head then indicated the two Overseers at the front.

"I do not trust these men," he growled.

"Well," said Doctaroo. "Technically it's just one man. But I take your point. I don't trust them either."

"In that case it is even more important that I protect you from them."

Doctaroo gave him a brilliant smile. "Aww, pet. That's so thoughtful of you."

She got up and gave him a hug. "Divvent you worry, hinnie," she said. "I've got the measure of those two. They'd have to get up pretty early in the morning to get the better of Doctaroo, I can tell you."

The train began to decelerate as it approached Blackfriars station, slowing to a halt as it reached the platform. There was no one around, so Henry opened the doors and they all disembarked as quietly as they could.

He approached a heavy steel door and tapped a code into the keypad next to it on the wall. With a hiss, the door slid upwards revealing behind it a white featureless corridor.

"This way," whispered Henry, walking cautiously into the corridor. The others followed him.

"How come there are no guards?" asked Doctaroo. "You'd think that in a top secret underground base there'd be some guards."

"We didn't think they were necessary," muttered The Overseer. "It's a top secret underground base. Nobody is supposed to know it exists."

They reached another door. Henry tapped in the code and it slid upwards to reveal yet more featureless corridor. This time however, there was an armed Kkrellem standing guard at the next door along.

"There," said The Overseer wryly. "Happy now?"

"Aye, champion," said Doctaroo happily. "That's much better. It feels like a proper top secret underground base now."

Kkrask stepped up. "I will talk to him," he said softly.

"Be careful, hinnie." Doctaroo said putting her hand on his arm. Kkrask gave her a broad grin.

"Do not worry Doctaroo. I am his superior, he has no option but to obey me."

Doctaroo raised an eyebrow. "I hope you're right, pet."

Kkrask moves off along the corridor. As he approached his compatriot, the other Kkrellem drew his blaster and pointed it at him. Kkrask stopped and raised a hand.

"Stow your weapon, Kkrail."

The other Kkrellem gave a smile of recognition and holstered the gun.

"Kkrask, when did you arrive? I had no word that you were coming." He looked down the corridor at the others. "Is that The Overseer?"

"Indeed," said Kkrask. "He wished to inspect the pipeline to ensure all was well."

"I see," said Kkrail. Then his face fell and he gave a serious frown. "I have some unfortunate news, my friend."

Kkrask raised an eyebrow. "Indeed? Explain."

"Your brother Kkrogh is dead." Kkrail said matter-of-factly.

Kkrask drew a breath. "Understood," he said calmly. "How did he die?"

"The human cow called Renifler shot him with a primitive projectile weapon. Death was instant. He did not suffer."

Kkrask took the news stoically. "Is Renifler still here?"

Kkrail nodded. "He is in the control room with Noor and another cow."

"And our brothers? What of them?"

"They have been confined to barracks," said Kkrail bitterly. "Only I and Kkorgh remain as guards."

The others, seeing that the Kkrellem on guard had put away his gun and seemed happy enough to see Kkrask, had approached them and were listening intently to their conversation. Doctaroo put her arm around Kkrask.

"I'm sorry about your brother," she said softly. "Were you close?"

Kkrask shook his head. "He was a boorish, bigoted bully," he said. "It was only a matter of time before *somebody* killed him."

Kkrail nodded vigorously. "Indeed, there have been many occasions where I myself came close to doing it."

Kkrask smiled sadly at Kkrail's enthusiasm. "Regardless of the feelings of others, he was still my brother and as the eldest of our brood, I am duty bound to avenge his death." He put both hands on Kkrail's shoulders.

"Will you join me, Kkrail?"

The big Kkrellem lifted his chin slightly and nodded.

"Need you ask?"

Kkrask smiled grimly. "Then muster our brothers Kkrail. We will need their help."

Kkrail opened the door.

"We must keep to the shadows. Noor has the main control room guarded by his other cows, but the path around its perimeter is clear. They have shut down most of the complex, allowing only for air and basic power requirements. Most of the energy from our vessel is being diverted to the control centre."

Kkrask was surprised at this.

258

"*Our* vessel?" he said. "But that is two hundred years in the past. How is he channelling its power?"

"Through the device you created for this human cow." Kkrail pointed to The Overseer.

The Overseer stepped forward.

"No, no, no. The gnu is just a MacGuffin. It has no purpose other than as a plot device. Without it, the title of this book makes no sense."

Kkrask looked sideways at him.

"But the blueprints you provided were for a power exchanger," he said.

"Yes, but only for localised use. All it was meant to do was to channel the geothermal energy into the pipeline to heat the water." The Overseer complained.

"The pipeline you were going to use to divert the superheated steam into cracks in the Earth's crust?" A loud Liverpudlian voice cut through the air like a rusty knife through a block of polystyrene.

Doctaroo spun round to see Beryl, Mr Walsh, Brian and Maule-Ffinch leading a small contingent of Royal Marines into the corridor.

"Well, you took your time!" grinned a jubilant Doctaroo.

"Yeah, well. We can't all be going off gallivanting through glowy vortex thingies." Beryl ran over and gave Doctaroo a hug.

"Aww, hinnie, it's so good to see you all," she shot a sly glance at Maule-Ffinch. "Even you, Nigel."

Maule-Ffinch patted her on the back. "Goodness, Doctaroo. Where on Earth have you been?" He spotted Henry lurking at the back. "And what the hell is *he* doing here?" he demanded. Maule-Ffinch made a move towards him, but Doctaroo stood in his way. Maule-Ffinch glared at her.

"That man tried to *kill* us, Doctaroo."

"I know, pet. And we'll get him for it later. Right now though, we need him."

Mr Walsh opened his mouth to speak, but Doctaroo silenced him with a raised finger.

"Look, I know you're probably wondering what I've been up to and I feel the same about you. But there's no time for a recap right now as we've a dénouement to get to and I don't want to over complicate things. It hard enough trying to keep tabs of all the different plotlines without adding to the problem. Is that okay with everyone?"

They all nodded in agreement.

"Good," said Doctaroo firmly. "Now let's get on with it."

The Overseer was deep in conversation with Kkrask and Kkrail in an attempt to ascertain the real purpose of the golden gnu

From what he could gather, ME2 had replaced the original blueprint with a new one of his own. Instead of converting geothermal energy, it would somehow connect to itself in a different time zone - and channel power from the crashed Kkrellem warship in 1819. This power would then be focussed by the pipeline, which contained not water but a gigantic toroidal, synthetic diamond that ME2 had commissioned from a company in China. The diamond itself was comprised of billions of smaller diamonds fused into one by the geothermal energy that The Overseer had originally envisioned using.

The power from the Kkrellem ship, once focussed and concentrated, would be used to give life to millions of AIDEs that ME2 had stored deep under the city of London.

"That's incredible!" exclaimed The Overseer. "Such a complex and devious plan. Wish *I'd* thought of it."

"Oh don't worry, knowing you, you probably will," said Doctaroo disparagingly.

"Now, now, Doctaroo. I'm here to help."

Doctaroo laughed bitterly. "Oh, aye? Really? Correct me if I'm wrong, but weren't you the one who was after world domination?"

The Overseer shook his head emphatically. "No, of course not," he said. "The South East of England was enough for me. I had a nice little retirement planned. Pretty little seaside cottage in Bedfordshire, yacht moored in Luton harbour. It would've been just perfect. Then bloody ME2 comes along and ruins it all!"

"Ooh, that sounds lovely," Doctaroo began, then she paused as the input from her ears was properly processed by her brain. The Overseer waited patiently until a minuscule flicker of realisation sparked deep within the recesses of her mind. He glanced at Henry who was willing that spark to ignite the flame of recognition that would lead Doctaroo to finally understand...

"Hang on," she said. There's no seaside in Bedfordshire. Come to think of it, there's no harbour in Luton either."

Both Overseers high fived each other. Henry checked his watch.

"Damn! One minute twenty six. You win," he said, handing over twenty quid to his past persona. The Overseer took the money and pocketed it with a self-satisfied, "thank you."

Doctaroo stuck her tongue out and made several obscene gestures at them, a couple were even from Earth.

"I've gotta say though, mate," said a perturbed Henry. "Losing to a drongo like Noor would have been a proper bummer, sure. But losing to his android copy?" He shook his head, ruefully. "That's the real kicker, mate. I'll tell you that for nothing."

Mr Walsh, who was walking behind them with Beryl, Brian and Maule-Ffinch (just in case you'd thought I'd forgotten about them), cleared his throat in a poor attempt at disguising the fact that he was trying to attract their attention.

"What's all this about Noor's android copy?" he asked with just the right level of curiosity to make it look as though he wasn't really that interested when in reality he was metaphorically bursting with questions.

The Overseer began to explain, with the occasional interruption from Henry and Doctaroo, about their encounter with Renifler at Noor's apartment and their subsequent discovery of his artificial origin.

When he had finished his tale, Brian gave a low whistle, while Mr Walsh and Maule-Ffinch exchanged shocked looks. Even Beryl was stunned into silence at the revelation of their discovery of the real Noor's corpse.

"Ewww," she said. "I'd hate to think of the state his shoes would be in after having Noor juice all over them."

Doctaroo held a hand up to her face and with the other, pointed at Kkrask who was still wearing Noor's overcoat. "He got that coat out of the closet," she mouthed to Beryl. "See that stain on the bottom?" She nodded knowingly. Beryl screwed up her nose.

"Ewwwww, stop it," she gagged, almost throwing up. "That is just *disgusting*!"

At the end of the corridor, they reached another steel shuttered door.

"This is the entrance to the primary control centre," said Kkrail. "The Kkrellem have been prohibited from entering, so it is guarded only by the artificial human cows."

He drew his lips back in a snarl, exposing his beautifully sharp teeth. "Their flesh is rank and tastes like engine coolant," he informed Kkrask. "I do not recommend it."

"I have warned you before of the dangers of drinking coolant," Kkrask said. "In large quantities it has been known to cause hallucinations and insanity."

"I do not drink it anymore," said Kkrail defensively. "There is a human drink which replicates the intoxication but with relatively fewer unpleasant side effects. It is called a Jägerbomb!"

Chapter Twenty-Two

Inside the primary control centre situated beneath the River Thames, the artificial life form known as ME2 leaned against the gantry that ran around the top of the vast space below and smiled a smile so full of smug self-satisfaction that you could put a suit on it and call it Piers Morgan.

Below him, busily checking readouts on the various control consoles that lined the walls of the hangar-like area, were a number of copies of Noor, Renifler, a few politicians, several premier league footballers, an actor or two and a few minor television personalities.

And Christopher Biggins. Although ME2 couldn't recall crafting one of those.

The centre of the enormous room housed what Renifler would no doubt call ME2's pièce de résistance. Although why the Renifler copies insisted on keeping the French accent, ME2 had no idea. The fact that as a duplicate of the original they really had no need of it because:

A. They had never actually *been* to France, let alone been raised there,

B. They were duplicates and could choose whatever accent they wanted to use and,

C. It really annoyed ME2.

This last point, thought ME2, was probably why they insisted on keeping it.

But, I digress - again.

The centre of the primary control centre held about a hundred thousand in-vitro maturation tubes of ME2's design, each one housing a single artificial person in various stages of gestation from foetus to fully grown adult.

The genetic material for these second-generation copies had been provided by some of the most important people on the planet who donated their cells in the mistaken belief that they were buying the ultimate in self-defence. An exact duplicate programmed to stand in for them in hazardous situations and act as a front for the metaphorical executioner's axe.

The artificial lifeform programme had first been proposed twenty years earlier by a research scientist at Liverpool University.

He developed it over the next ten years before suddenly signing over the patent to the Metropolitan police. He had been found a few months later tied to a stake in a farmer's field disguised as a scarecrow. The body was only discovered when the farmer realised that he didn't have a scarecrow and even if he did, then he certainly wouldn't bother putting it up in a field he regularly used as a campsite in the summer months to earn an extra income.

Meanwhile, the Met's secret research laboratories had managed to create the first fully aware, artificial human that could be programmed not only to obey the commands of its 'owner', but who had the ability to learn.

The first AIDEs, those of the Met's Chief Constable, the Home Secretary and a young up and comer called Cedric Carstairs, were activated amid much pomp and ceremony, at a gala dinner in the Met's honour, thrown by the fellows of the Royal Society.

The three copies worked perfectly.

But, as the Met would discover to its cost, they worked a little too perfectly.

ME1 was the first of the three originals to realise how superior it was compared with the master pattern. Carstairs was a joke. A laughing stock so insignificant that they had to invent a special task force for him to command because he kept screwing up his previous assignments. His rate of turnover for new partners was the highest in the Met so rather than assign him a new one, they commissioned an artificial lifeform of Carstairs to be his latest partner.

It didn't take ME1 long to work out that he surpassed Carstairs in pretty much every way possible. To ensure that Carstairs gradually developed a healthy alcohol dependency was fairly simple. To gradually replace his double in his day to day life was pretty easy.

ME2 yawned. The day was finally catching up with him and he was incredibly tired. Allowing the original Renifler to live after he had assassinated ME1 was probably something ME2 would eventually regret, but for the moment, ME2 considered him an amusement and was content to allow Renifler's plans to play out just to see what would happen. Besides, he could always kill him later if necessary.

ME2 made a mental note to adjust the level of intelligence in the new batch of AIDEs. A little lower, perhaps and maybe reduce the level of autonomy to make them more obedient and less inclined to make important decisions without consulting him first. Noor2 was too much like his

271

template in that he possessed the same arrogance and delusions of grandeur that the real Johar Noor had in bucketfuls. ME2 gripped the rail tightly. He had never taken the life of one of his own kind before, but he was beginning to wonder if it was time to change that. He looked down at the 'factory floor' where Noor2 was busy directing the duplicates in their duties. He stopped one of them, ME2 seemed to recognise him, Daniel Radcliffe he thought. Noor2 began to berate the confused young man and then started to beat him savagely.

ME2 had had enough. He drew Carstairs gun, took aim and then shot Noor2 in the head. Noor2 fell backwards and hit the floor with a wet thump. Daniel Radcliffe looked up at the gantry. ME2 stared back.

"Get on with your work," he called down. "And call a clean-up crew to take care of that." He pointed at the fresh corpse which was gradually leaking red fluid all over the concrete floor.

Daniel Radcliffe nodded and went off to carry out his orders.

A vent in the ceiling dropped open on its hinge and Lt. Morris poked his head through and took a quick look around. He pulled his head back in and a moment later he hung down, legs first and dropped as quietly as he could onto the gantry, followed by the rest of his men.

"Spread out," he whispered. "Cover the area." He took out his radio.

"Mr Maule-Ffinch? We are in position." There was a crackle from the radio.

"Jolly good," came the reply. "Erm, could you just hold the line for a minute please?"

Morris frowned. "Is everything okay down there?"

He was answered with static.

Maule-Ffinch held the radio in his left hand but his attention was diverted by the Glock held in the right hand of Carstairs' double, ME2. He raised an eyebrow when he saw Doctaroo standing with the two Overseers.

"Well, well, well," he said with a cheery grin. "I never expected to see you again, Doctaroo. I thought Henry had finally got rid of you for good."

Surreptitiously, Henry reached into his trouser pocket for his TEI. Noticing this, The Overseer moved over to disguise Henry's movements.

"Cat got your tongue, Doctaroo?" asked ME2. There was still no reply. Mr Walsh coughed and poked Doctaroo in her side. She flinched and looked up from her phone. She lifted a hand to an ear and removed a wireless ear bud from it.

"Sorry," she said. "I was listening to that Lewis Capaldi fella's new album. It's proper good an' all."

ME2 was about to comment when suddenly, Henry jumped to one side and pointed a small box at him.

"Don't move!" Henry shouted.

ME2 gave him a quizzical look. "That's a packet of Rothmans King Size," he said. "I don't smoke, thanks all the same."

"Bugger!" Shouted Henry and jumped back behind his former self.

"Okay, the next person to move gets shot," said ME2. "And in case you don't believe me..."

He pointed the gun at Brian, pulled the trigger and shot him straight between the eyes. Brian fell dead to the ground and Beryl screamed. Mr Walsh was too shocked to move and Doctaroo looked sadly at the body of her companion. She turned her gaze to ME2 and it grew cold and hard with suppressed anger.

"You've just made the biggest mistake ever," she hissed, all trace of her usual frivolity gone. "I am seriously going to kick the fu..."

"Be quiet," said ME2. He opened the door behind him and several of his AIDEs marched out to meet him. Maule-Ffinch whispered to Mr Walsh.

"Isn't that David Beckham?" he asked."

"Yeah," Mr Walsh replied. "And that one is Idris Elba."

"Quiet!" said ME2. He waved his men forwards. "Take them to the very big conference room and lock them in."

The AIDEs began to herd them down the corridor. Doctaroo shot ME2 a final look of pure hatred before putting an arm around a distraught Beryl's shoulders.

"There, there hinnie. Don't you fret, I'll get the bas..."

"But what if you don't?" wailed Beryl.

"Of course we will," she said as they rounded the corner out of view of ME2. "Won't we, Idris?"

"Sure will, Doctaroo!" said the big man by her side, before punching the AIDE next to him and knocking him out.

Mr Walsh was agog. "Bloody hell!" he exclaimed. "You mean he's the real..."

"Idris Elba, yes," smiled Doctaroo. "We're old, er, pals. I phoned him from Noor's apartment earlier, didn't I pet?"

Idris Elba nodded. "Yeah. I reached out to my mates at MI5 and they managed to sneak me in as my own copy."

"MI5?" Maule-Ffinch was confused.

276

"Oh, aye. Idris is one of their top agents." Doctaroo explained. "The acting thing is only a cover. In fact, his name isn't really Idris Elba."

"Really? What is it then?" asked Mr Walsh.

"Frank. Frank Higginbottom," said Idris Elba.

"I can see why you changed it," said Beryl.

Idris Elba looked around. "Look, we haven't much time. If you're gonna pull some miracle out of your hat, Doctaroo, now's the time to do it."

Nigel Maule-Ffinch smiled. "I think I can help you there, Mr Elba," he said taking a walkie-talkie from his pocket. He held it up and pressed the call button.

"Kkrask, it's Maule-Ffinch. Are you in position?"

The radio crackled and Kkrask's voice came over the comms. "Indeed, we are ready."

"Lieutenant Morris, are you and your men ready?"

"We are awaiting your signal, sir."

Maule-Ffinch's eyes narrowed and his jaw was set.

"Then let's go to work," he said grimly.

Chapter Twenty-Three

In the primary control centre there was a party. Human guests mingled with their AIDE counterparts, laughing and joking with each other and generally having a very nice time.

Her Majesty the Queen was being shown around by a now sober, DCI Carstairs who was none the wiser as to what was really going on. Still thinking that the Queen was there to formally dedicate London's new clean energy power station, he completely missed the fact that, for the most part, the guests were MPs, heads of state and people in positions of power. He completely missed the fact that each of them suddenly seemed to have their own AIDE double and, perhaps most importantly of all, he completely missed the fact that Dr Noor was nowhere to be seen and that the whole shebang appeared to be run by Carstairs' *own* copy, ME2.

There was one moment when a fleeting thought crossed his mind about how odd things seemed, but that was swiftly nipped in the bud by yet another glass of Cristal pressed into his hand by the ever present, smiling waitress.

ME2 watched the inspector impassively. He was constantly amazed at how easily manipulated human beings were, especially when it was assisted by certain chemicals introduced into their bloodstream disguised as alcohol.

The plan had been ME1's originally. Replace every important person, be they heads of state, politician or celebrity with AIDE copies under his control. World domination made easy. In fact, for a fleeting moment ME2 seriously considered writing an autobiography using that as its title. Then he stopped being silly.

ME1 had first travelled to India to find a suitable candidate to use as a patsy and had provided him with the identity of Dr Johar Noor, billionaire philanthropist and tech genius, ensuring that records, databases and social media held all the information they required to convince those who needed convincing that the Noor was who he was told to claim to be. Noor in turn had hired Renifler and then deliberately attracted the attention of The Overseer, who was already known by Scotland Yard, who provided him with the actual technical knowledge and money he needed to build the pipeline.

Unfortunately, ME1 had begun to show alarming character flaws, the most glaring was that he was a raging psychopath. It was when he had contacted the Home Office and they had brought in

Doctaroo, who happened to be The Overseer's arch foe, that ME2 made the decision to use Renifler to take ME1 out of the picture. This way he was certain that the DCI would "activate" *him* to run the investigation. So far, things were going perfectly to plan. Well, perhaps not *perfectly*. But as well as they could, all things considered.

He was about to make a start with the dedication ceremony, when canisters of tear gas dropped from the gantry above, began to spew out their noxious, choking contents. The humans ran for cover, while the AIDEs stood still and waited for further instructions, the gas having little to no visible effect on them.

As the guests reached the exits, they found them locked and their way barred by more AIDEs. Unsure of what to do next, they huddled together in fear.

DCI Carstairs had accompanied Her Majesty to Noor's private exit on the opposite side of the room. He was reaching for the handle when the door burst inwards to reveal an armoured and fully armed Kkrellem warrior. At the same time, every other door burst open to reveal similarly armed Kkrellem who advanced on the AIDEs, ray guns and swords held aloft. With a yell, several Royal Marines rappelled down ropes to the control centre's floor, firing their guns at any AIDE who dared to shoot first.

ME2 had evacuated as soon as the first shots were fired and was hurrying to the secondary control room. As he got there, he was startled to see the imposing figure of Idris Elba step from the shadows. He was bloody astonished to see that he was accompanied by Doctaroo and her friends.

"Going somewhere, pet?" she asked.

ME2 stepped back and drew Carstairs' gun from his belt. "Stand back, Doctaroo. I have absolutely no qualms about using this."

"You killed my friend," she said softly. "I'm a bit upset about that."

"I'm sorry," ME2 said with very heavy sarcasm. "I'm afraid you must have me confused with someone who gives a fu..."

He staggered back suddenly, as Idris Elba's fist made contact with his stomach and he fell winded to the ground.

Maule-Ffinch stepped up. "Brian. His name is Brian."

"Was Brian, you mean," corrected ME2. Idris Elba punched him again.

You're going to let us into your control room," Mr Walsh knelt next to him and whispered into his ear. "Or I'm gonna let Idris here work out all his frustrations on your face."

ME2 laughed and spat a gobbet of bright pink liquid on the floor.

"Go ahead," he said casually. "It will have little to no effect on me as my pain receptors we're disabled the moment I first came online."

Mr Walsh stood up and switched places with Beryl.

"My mate Lieutenant Morris says that the door is locked by both a palm print and a retina print." She held up a penknife. And gave a smile that was half sneer, half triumphant grin. "So you see, we don't actually need *all* of you in order to open it."

ME2's cockiness vanished to be replaced by mild curiosity.

"Interesting," he said calmly. "I wonder if you have the courage to do it yourself."

Lieutenant Morris knelt down next to her and took the penknife. He looked ME2 right in the eye.

"It doesn't matter," he said. "I have enough courage for both of us."

ME2 sighed resignedly. "In that case, Lieutenant, it seems I have little option but to open the door."

He got to his feet and placed his right hand on the panel by the door. There was a series of bleeps and clicks and a small camera style iris opened just above the palm print reader.

ME2 put his right eye against the iris and the door slid upwards to reveal Renifler, holding an HK MP5 sub-machine gun which he subsequently fired, spraying bullets into the corridor.

Kkrask, Kkrail and a dozen or so of their fellow Kkrellem warriors were assisting the Marines in clearing up after the party.

"You know," Kkrail said munching on an arm, "these duplicates don't taste so bad when you get used to them."

"That doesn't belong to a duplicate," said Kkrask pointing at a wheeled stretcher where an ashen faced Christopher Biggins was being treated by one of the newly arrived paramedics. Kkrail put down the arm.

"Do you think it is too late for them to re-attach it?" he asked hopefully.

"Considering the human has lost it at the shoulder and you are chewing the flesh from its elbow, I would say yes. It is."

Kkrail grinned showing a mouthful of very sharp teeth. "In that case, I might as well finish it off!" he said happily. Kkrask returned the smile.

"Save me the thumb," he said. "I fancy drying and maple smoking it."

"Ahhh, jerky!" said Kkrail. "I haven't had human cow jerky in many a cycle."

DCI Carstairs approached them slowly. Kkrask drew his gun.

"Don't shoot," cried Carstairs. "I'm not my AIDE."

Kkrask holstered his weapon. "You are the one they call Kkarstairs?"

The DCI nodded. "Yes."

"You are not required here," announced Kkrask. "Doctaroo has taken charge."

"Doctaroo?" shouted Carstairs in surprise. "Doctaroo is in charge? She couldn't charge a bloody battery!"

Kkrask ignored him. "Would you like me to take you to her?"

Carstairs gulped as he took note of the big Kkrellem's muscles and sharp teeth.

"Yes," he said quietly. "Yes please."

"Very well, human. Follow me."

Chapter Twenty-Four

Doctaroo and the others ducked as the bullets from Renifler's gun went over their heads hitting the wall behind them, the distraction allowing Renifler and ME2 to escape. Morris and Idris Elba gave chase, while Doctaroo, Mr Walsh, Beryl, Maule-Ffinch and the two Overseers walked slowly into the now dark and empty secondary control centre. Henry ran over to the central console and typed into its keyboard.

"I can stop the power transfer temporarily from here," he said as he flicked switches and spun dials. "But it really needs to be shut down from the other end to really stop it."

"You mean from 1819?" Doctaroo said.

"Well, yes," said Henry. "Hey, Doctaroo, that's two things you guessed correctly today! Nice one!"

Doctaroo beamed. "I know," she said happily. "If I keep on like this they'll *have* to let me back in."

"Who's that, Doctaroo?" asked Maule-Ffinch. "Mensa? The Royal Society?"

"No, pet," said Doctaroo. "Ashington Library. They took my card off me 'cos I kept taking out Fifty Shades of Grey."

"Well, that's nothing to be ashamed of, apparently lots of people have read it."

"Aye, but I thought it was a DIY manual," said Doctaroo quietly.

"So do a lot of people!" cackled Beryl and she and Doctaroo collapsed into laughter.

"Okay," said Mr Walsh trying to bring some semblance of order back into the proceedings. "How are we gonna shut the damn thing off in 1819? Does anyone have a handy dandy time machine on them?"

"Aye pet," said Doctaroo, "and here he comes now."

She indicated the doorway to the secondary control centre which was now filled by the huge frame of Kkrask. From behind him Kkrail poked his snout over his shoulder and for a second, Beryl could have sworn she saw what looked like the tip of someone's finger sticking out from between his teeth. Behind Kkrail, jumping up to make himself seen was DCI Carstairs.

Maule-Ffinch soon brought them up to speed and both Kkrellem agreed to use the mirror vortex to return to 1819.

"You should take Robert back with you," said Doctaroo. "And him too." She jerked a thumb at The Overseer.

"Now hang on a minute," said Carstairs. "From what I can gather, he's the one responsible for all this! I've just had to send the bloody Queen back to Buckingham Palace in a bloody Uber! Bang goes my knighthood."

"Actually, Inspector," said Maule-Ffinch. "He's not. The people really responsible for what's happened today are Dr Noor," he levelled his gaze at the Inspector, "and you."

"What?" To say that Carstairs was taken aback by this would be as understated as saying that the Symphony of the Seas, currently the world's largest cruise ship, was a nice little dinghy.

"Yes." Maule-Ffinch said calmly. "Well, seeing as he is technically you, I'm therefore holding *you* personally responsible for his actions, in particular the cold-blooded murder of someone we all held in very high esteem. But since we don't actually have ME2 in custody, the person whose vanity caused the creation of not one, but *two* identical copies of himself using alien technology, will suffice.

"But these two people are responsible *for* the alien technology Noor used to create the AIDEs in the first place." Carstairs protested.

The Overseer gave his best innocent look. "Actually, we only provided the technological know-how to build the pipeline. We had no idea what your double and Noor planned to use it for."

"But you were going to use the pipeline to cause earthquakes in London!" Carstairs exclaimed. We found it all in the blueprints on..." his voice tailed off.

"On where, Inspector?" Asked Henry.

Carstairs liked dry lips. "On the disk we found in Noor's house."

It is at this point, mainly because it's the end of this book and protracted endings bore me slightly, I would like to impart the following information.

Lieutenant Morris and Idris Elba returned having lost ME2 and Renifler. Maule-Ffinch then had them arrest Carstairs (I never liked him anyway, a middle aged man with a ponytail? Really?).

Kkrask and the other Kkrellem returned to the nineteenth century along with Robert Stephenson (I know, right?) and The Overseer.

What subsequently happened to them is an adventure for another time.

Henry was sent back to his cottage in Bonny Scotland, where he occasionally works for the Home Office under the auspices of Nigel Maule-Ffinch.

Doctaroo, Beryl and Mr Walsh were taken back to Scotland Yard where they were reunited with Doctaroo's Trydis. After saying their goodbyes (and after a five course dinner at The Ritz courtesy of a grateful Home Secretary), she opened the door of the phone box.

Beryl stopped and gazed sadly at the city skyline. "I miss Brian."

"We all do, hinnie," said Doctaroo. "But I'll promise you this, pet. I'm not going to rest until

I bring his murderer to justice." She yawned. "First, though, I'm gonna go and have forty winks. I don't know about you, but I'm knackered."

The three friends entered the ship and the door slammed shut after them. With the indescribable noise alluded to earlier in the story, the Trydis took off and Doctaroo, Mr Walsh and Beryl flew off to new adventures.

Idris Elba returned to Hollywood where he starred in many quality movies.

And Prometheus.

Christopher Biggins wasn't harmed in the writing of this book.

Epilogue

He was in the back of a van that much was
clear. Partly because of the sound of a diesel engine,
partly because of the heavy bang as the double doors
were slammed shut once he'd been bundled inside, a
thick black hood over his head. But he mainly knew

that he was in a van because the two men, one of whom had a thick French accent, kept arguing about how the Frenchman had stolen the wrong make of van. Apparently he'd taken a Renault Traffic when the other man had stipulated that he obtain a Ford Transit.

After what seemed like hours, the van had stopped and the men had dragged him out and into some sort of building. They had sat him in a chair and one of them had removed the hood.

ME2 looked closely at his captive's face, Renifler stood guard holding the HK close to him like it was a baby.

ME2 smiled gently.

"Hello Brian," he said softly. "I bet you're wondering where you are…"

www.ingramcontent.com/pod-product-compliance
Lightning Source LLC
Chambersburg PA
CBHW071308200626
46813CB00015B/647